USA TODAY BESTSELLING AUTHOR

RITA HERRON

SAFE BY HIS SIDE

MANHUNT **2** SERIES

Beachside Reads
Norcross, GA 30092

Cover Design: Jeffery Olsen
Cover Photo: The Illustrated Romance, https://illustratedromance.com
Print Design: Dayna Linton, Day Agency
eBook Interior Design: Dayna Linton, Day Agency

ISBN: 978-1-949178-02-9 (Paperbook)
ISBN: 978-1-949178-03-6 (eBook)

Third Edition: 2018

10 9 8 7 6 5 4 3

Printed in the USA

To my mother who never read until I wrote my first book!

I miss you every day, Mother.

Love,
Rita

SAFE BY HIS SIDE

PROLOGUE

THE DARKNESS CLOSED AROUND Lenora Lockhart. Suffocating. Endless.

The four-by-four room where her abductor kept her gave her no room to move. To stretch.

No way to escape.

God knows she'd tried everything. Had torn her nails and skin clawing at the heavy cement and wood door. Her wrists had bled from her attempts to free herself of the chains. And the rest of her body ached from . . . fighting him.

She had no idea where she was. What city or state.

Only that she'd been here for weeks. At first, she'd tried counting the days and hours, but with no clock or window, she'd lost track of time completely. She wasn't even sure when it was daylight.

Except—the night was when he came.

Footsteps sounded, creating a shuffling noise as he dragged his limp foot behind him. Next to her, another woman's sobs wrenched the air as he opened the door to her prison.

Lenora's own terror vibrated in the dankness as she struggled for a breath. She buried her head against her legs, her throat thick with fear as she listened to the woman scream.

Hating that she couldn't save her, Lenora shoved her fist against her mouth to stop herself from yelling at him to stop. If she did, he'd drag her in the room and force her to watch.

He'd done it before.

And as much as the woman's cries sickened her, she'd learned to be quiet. Follow his orders.

It was the only way to survive.

And she was going to survive, dammit.

She had too much to live for. Her mother was probably hysterical wondering where she was. If she was alive.

And her fiancé . . . their wedding plans . . . they'd just started making them. Her bridal gown was in the shop for alterations. The lilies had been ordered. The food and DJ arranged . . .

Her chest heaved. Drew was probably crazy with worry as well.

She glanced down at her tattered clothes, dirty and blood-stained, and knew she looked horrible. Didn't want him to see her like this . . .

Would Drew still love her when he heard what this bastard had done to her?

The rancid smell of sweat, urine, and vomit permeated the

air from the icy chambers. Her own sweat, now mixed with his. Her own fear and body odors. Her skin felt clammy, dirty, her mouth gritty, dry.

The screams grew louder, and she squeezed her eyes shut, but the images of what he was doing to his other captive flashed in front of her eyes like a horror show.

Her stomach convulsed, and she swallowed hard to hold back the bile rising to her throat.

Suddenly though, the screams died. A huffed breath reverberated in the air. A curse. Then bitter, sinister laughter.

Had he killed her?

If so, that meant she'd be next . . .

A loud noise exploded from somewhere. Upstairs? Were they in the basement of a house? A cave?

Voices shouted, footsteps clattered, then her captor cursed. She heard his shuffling as he raced past her door. Where was he going? Not up the stairs?

Was there a hidden exit down here?

More voices, shouts, footsteps, then the sound of something breaking. Wood? A body slamming against the door to the upstairs?

"Police!"

"Stop, it's over!"

A gunshot rang out. More footsteps.

She held her breath, wiping at the tears running down her face. She was going to be rescued. Free at last . . .

Another gunshot.

"I've got the bastard!" a man shouted.

"Look for the women!" a female yelled.

"Dammit to hell. This one's dead," the man said. "And still warm. If we'd only gotten here sooner."

A rush of emotions overwhelmed Lenora, and she beat at the door. "Help! I'm in here!" She balled her sore hands into fists and pounded as hard as she could.

Seconds later, the man with the deep voice shouted, "Stand back. I'm going to get you out."

She backed into the dark corner as far as she could, a shudder coursing through her as she heard him trying to open the door. Metal ground against wood, the sound of an ax slamming against something.

Finally, the door screeched open. A faint stream of light nearly blinded her, and she squinted, her vision blurred, her memory foggy. How many days had it been since she'd been let out of the darkness?

Not since he'd brought her here.

Pain shot through her temple as the light of a flashlight hit her eyes. "I've got a live one!" the man with the deep voice shouted.

More footsteps pounded as if they were racing through the place searching for others. Lenora shivered, emotions overwhelming her as her rescuer lowered the flashlight and shined it on the floor of her prison.

"My name is Sergeant Micah Hardin with the Texas Rangers, Miss. I'm here to save you."

She nodded, but her body felt frozen. Too many times the other man had come for her. Dragged her out. Done unspeakable things to her.

Could she trust this man?

He'd said he was police, hadn't he?

"You're Lenora Lockhart, aren't you?"

Relief whirled inside her. He knew her name.

"I won't hurt you," he said in a husky murmur. "We've been looking for you and the others for a long time." He dropped to his knees, crawling into the cave-like darkness with her.

The glint of metal flashed in front of her, and she realized he was showing her his badge. "See, the Silver Star of Texas. Sergeant Micah Hardin."

He held his hand out to her. "Come on, you're safe now. Let me help you."

Fear mingled with humiliation at the condition she was in. But she finally tore her arms from around her legs, took his hand and crawled from her prison.

Shadows moved. Her captor bellowed as a lawman hauled him up and handcuffed him.

She choked on a sob as the sergeant helped her to stand. But she was so weak that she collapsed against him.

He swung her up into his arms, and she buried her head against his chest as he carried her through the dark tunnel, then up the steps and out into the night away from the horror.

Five years later

THE LAST THING SERGEANT Micah Hardin wanted to do today was to have to tell Lenora Lockhart that Robert Simpleton, the man who'd abducted and brutalized her, had escaped from prison.

But she had to know because most likely Simpleton would come after her.

He cursed as he drove toward the outskirts of Austin where she'd moved after Simpleton's trial.

She'd been battered and traumatized from her captivity, but still, she'd summoned enough courage to face the bastard in court and name every horrific thing she'd endured.

Then her fiancé had left her.

Son of a bitch. How could he have walked away from such a brave, gutsy woman and the life they'd planned together?

Lenora hadn't deserved the abuse Simpleton had inflicted on her. And she sure as hell hadn't deserved for the man who'd professed to love her to abandon her when she'd needed him most.

Not that Lenora was his problem. She'd been a case. Nothing more.

Except . . . he'd found her in that awful, filthy boxlike room and felt the terror quivering through her when he'd carried her out into the light to safety.

He'd seen a lot of sick assholes in his day, but Simpleton was one of the worst. As much as he'd tried to steel himself against the gruesome details, his heart had ached for Lenora.

At least she had survived. Although experience told him

that some victims preferred death to the trauma of living a life after the hell they'd endured.

What about Lenora? Was she still suffering? Had she managed to put her nightmares to rest and move on with her life?

Sweat exploded on his brow as guilt assaulted him.

If she had, he was about to destroy that sense of peace.

Dammit to hell, the sadist and the other two prisoners who'd escaped the state pen should never have been allowed visitors or mail. Because they had to have had help from the outside to plan their escape.

Of course, that help could have come from the inside. Other prisoners' contacts, security officers, chow hall staff, even counselors could be bought with money or sympathy.

For the life of him, he couldn't figure out why anyone would feel sorry for Robert Simpleton or the other two men because they'd committed heinous crimes against women.

The FBI was investigating the prison employees and inmates now. Even the warden had fallen under intense scrutiny.

Thankfully one of the prisoners Geoffrey Jones had been found. A Texas Ranger had beaten the feds to him and killed the bastard.

He chuckled. Sometimes the feds and Rangers fought over jurisdiction. But this time they'd welcomed the help. Dangerous prisoners on the loose tended to cause panic, and there had been four murders inside the prison in one month, meaning the FBI had their work cut out there.

Ranches and farmland sprawled across the terrain, reminding him of his own spread outside Austin. Lenora would need a safe place to hide until they caught Simpleton.

What would she think about going to his ranch with him?

An image of Lenora in his home taunted him. Lenora in his kitchen sipping coffee and sharing breakfast with him. Lenora outside riding across his land . . .

Jesus, he could not go there, could not start thinking about her in a personal way.

His job was to protect her and find Simpleton, not get involved with her.

Or fantasize about having her for himself.

No, detective work and relationships didn't mix.

He'd make sure Lenora was safe until Simpleton was back in the pen—or dead—then he'd leave her in peace again so she could find the happiness Simpleton had stolen from her.

LENORA ADJUSTED THE DISPLAY of wedding veils hanging by the floor length mirror, then moved on to straighten the shoe rack before rehanging the dresses Edie Nivens had spent the morning trying on.

Finally, the young bride-to-be had chosen a white strapless, sweetheart gown with lacy overlays. Lenora had taken her measurements for alterations and ordered shoes and the veil Edie had wanted.

Edie had left happy, relaxed and chattering nonstop about her upcoming big day.

A sliver of sadness threatened to destroy Lenora's good

mood, but she tamped it down. Her mother and everyone else who'd known her before the attack thought she was crazy for opening a bridal shop when her own nuptials had been called off so suddenly.

When her heart had been broken.

But she'd rebelled against sympathy and the pitying stares—she'd endured too much of that after her abduction and the trial where she'd had to bare her soul in public.

So she'd chosen to dive into a career that would allow her to at least experience joy through others' happiness.

Just because she hadn't found true love and her happily-ever-after and didn't expect to, didn't mean that she couldn't enjoy helping others have that special day.

Truth was, the bridal shop had been cathartic for her. Too long she'd lived in that dark world, undergoing therapy, reliving the nightmares as she relayed details of her ordeal to lawyers and counselors, and then reading about her experiences in the paper the following day.

She had survived. But not without major scars, mostly invisible to others. The nightmares still tormented her at night. The demons and shadows still haunted her. The fear . . . threatened to immobilize her at the most unexpected times.

But she refused to succumb to that fear and let it paralyze her. Focusing on the darkness would rob her sanity.

And that would be a win for the sick bastard who'd hurt her.

Her assistant, Jenny Beal, flipped the closed sign on the front store door, then turned to her with a smile. "Whew. What a busy day."

"June is the big month for weddings." Which meant that brides-to-be had to order their dresses and start planning in the summer and fall. Rush jobs made everything more stressful and created unnecessary problems.

"Go on home," Lenora said. "I'll stay and finish for the day."

Jenny beamed a smile. "Thanks, Lenora. My boyfriend said he had plans for us tonight."

Lenora's heart fluttered. "You think he's going to propose?"

Jenny's green eyes lit up. "I don't know. I hope so!" She laughed, then practically bounced across the room in her excitement, her ponytail bobbing as she slung her purse over her shoulder and rushed out the back door.

Lenora watched her leave with a mixture of emotions. Joy for the twenty-three-year-old filled her. Even though she was only twenty-eight herself, she felt old. Ancient.

Hardened. Jaded.

And . . . lonely.

Had she ever been that naive and full of dreams?

Yes . . . before Robert Simpleton.

But he was locked away now and she was safe. That was all that mattered.

Sighing, she walked over to the cash register, tallied up the money and receipts for the day, then removed the credit card slips and checks and put them in the safe in her office. Tomorrow she'd make a bank deposit, but tonight she had a date with a bubble bath.

A noise sounded from the back, and she startled. Damn her nerves. It was probably just Jenny coming back for something.

She was notorious for forgetting her keys.

She headed to the double doors leading to the back, but a knock on the front door made her jump.

Irritated with herself for being so jittery, she turned and walked to the front, then peered through the glass expecting to see Jenny.

But her breath caught at the sight of a man on the front stoop.

Not just any man. Sgt. Micah Hardin.

Memories flooded her. The dark prison room, his deep voice calling to her, his warm hand clasping hers and pulling her out, his strong arms carrying her to safety and into the light.

She'd had such a difficult time and hadn't trusted anyone but him back then, so the prosecutor had asked him to stay throughout the trial. His soft reassurances as he'd supported her through her testimony had saved her.

The familiar sting of tears, panic and fear seized her. She hadn't seen the Texas Ranger in years.

There was only one reason she could think of that he was here now.

Robert Simpleton must be out of jail.

And if he was, he was on his way to find her and kill her.

MICAH'S GUT CLENCHED AT the instant fear that snapped into Lenora's eyes as she opened the door to her bridal shop.

Had she already heard about the prison escape?

Feminine scents suffused him as he stepped inside, the sight of dozens of bridal gowns, veils, shoes, and accessories striking him as ironic. He'd heard Lenora had opened a wedding shop and thought it odd since her fiancé had dumped her before the trial.

But an image of Lenora in the satin sheath hanging in front of the mirror to the right hit him, and his aching heart skipped a beat.

"Micah," she said in a throaty whisper. "You should have called."

"I wanted to see you in person." *And offer my services to protect you.*

She crossed her arms, her delicate jaw tightening just enough for him to see that she was nervous and trying to hide it. He'd noticed the same telltale signs at the trial.

Then he'd managed to soothe her because Simpleton was in custody.

Now . . .

"What happened?" she asked, her eyes searching his.

He wanted to lie and tell her that he'd just been in the area and thought he'd drop by and check on her. But he couldn't do that and protect her.

"Three prisoners broke out of the state pen," he said bluntly. "I'm afraid Robert Simpleton was one of them."

Robert Simpleton ripped off his prison uniform in the bathroom, grinning as he looked down at the initials he'd carved on his upper arm.

LL. Lenora Lockhart.

A vision of blond loveliness that had fueled his wet dreams in prison for the last few years. He wanted to touch her, hold her, shove his dick down her throat and inside her.

Make her pay for what she'd done to him.

All this time he'd done without a woman because of that bitch.

He yanked on the T-shirt and jeans his friend had stashed in the car for him, then pulled out the mustache and sideburns kit and began creating his disguise.

Lenora would remember the scraggly locks of hair that he once had, but she wouldn't recognize the shaved and totally tattooed head that was now his signature. The snakes that crawled across his bald head wrapped around a skeleton's bones.

Twenty minutes later, he eyed his new look in the mirror with a grin and admired the artwork that adorned his entire body.

Someone knocked on the door, then his friend's voice called his name.

"You about ready, Robert?"

He chuckled to himself. Keeping in good with Cissy had been a smart move on his part. Cissy had always wanted him.

He opened the door and hauled her inside. Her startled yelp turned to a sultry smile as he tore her shirt off, lowered his mouth and sucked her tits.

"God, Robert, I've wanted you for so long," she whispered.

She smelled like sweat, cigarettes, and booze, the latter two nearly making him gag. Lenora had smelled feminine, like lavender and sweetness, the way a woman should.

At least she had when he'd first abducted her.

Cissy ran her tongue across his jaw and anger sparked inside him. He didn't want her.

He wanted Lenora.

But Cissy ripped down his zipper and shoved at his pants, then closed her hand around his dick, and he groaned. If he didn't hurry, he was going to come all over her hand. He'd had enough hand jobs in prison.

Breath heaving, he spun her around, pushed her up against the bathroom wall, shoved her skirt up and gripped her hips. She wore black panties that he ripped with one hand, then he thrust his bulging cock inside her.

She groaned his name, clawing at the wall as he fucked her senseless. Their bodies slammed against each other, sweat sliding against sweat, his cock ramming harder and harder until he exploded inside her.

His cum dripped down her legs as he pulled out.

"I love you," she whispered. "Now we can finally be together."

Disgust filled him at the sight of her. Instead, Lenora's beautiful face flashed in his mind, taunting him.

Cissy might have wanted him forever. But he had other plans for his future.

A future that didn't involve her.

She twisted in his arms, smiling as she turned to face him,

her tits red and swollen from his mouth, her eyes still glazed with passion.

And the promise of more.

But there would be no more for her. She'd served her purpose.

He slid one hand down and retrieved the pocketknife she'd included in the duffel bag, flipped it open and slit her throat.

Her gasp of pain and shock made his cock harden again, and he stroked himself as he watched the blood drain from her. Then he carefully carved the X between her breasts. He wanted to mark her as he had his other victims. Wanted the world to know that he was back.

Satisfied, he dropped her lifeless body to the floor, yanked his pants back up, grabbed the duffel bag, and stuffed the toiletry kit inside.

The clock was ticking, the minutes passing. The cops would be looking for him. They might warn Lenora he was coming.

But he'd find a way to get her.

To have her.

And this time no one would stop him.

CHAPTER 1

Five years later

THE LAST THING SERGEANT Micah Hardin wanted to do today was to have to tell Lenora Lockhart that Robert Simpleton, the man who'd abducted and brutalized her, had escaped from prison.

But she had to know because most likely Simpleton would come after her.

He cursed as he drove toward the outskirts of Austin where she'd moved after Simpleton's trial.

She'd been battered and traumatized from her captivity, but still, she'd summoned enough courage to face the bastard in court and name every horrific thing she'd endured.

Then her fiancé had left her.

Son of a bitch. How could he have walked away from such a brave, gutsy woman and the life they'd planned together?

Lenora hadn't deserved the abuse Simpleton had inflicted on her. And she sure as hell hadn't deserved for the man who'd professed to love her to abandon her when she'd needed him most.

Not that Lenora was his problem. She'd been a case. Nothing more.

Except . . . he'd found her in that awful, filthy boxlike room and felt the terror quivering through her when he'd carried her out into the light to safety.

He'd seen a lot of sick assholes in his day, but Simpleton was one of the worst. As much as he'd tried to steel himself against the gruesome details, his heart had ached for Lenora.

At least she had survived. Although experience told him that some victims preferred death to the trauma of living a life after the hell they'd endured.

What about Lenora? Was she still suffering? Had she managed to put her nightmares to rest and move on with her life?

Sweat exploded on his brow as guilt assaulted him.

If she had, he was about to destroy that sense of peace.

Dammit to hell, the sadist and the other two prisoners who'd escaped the state pen should never have been allowed visitors or mail. Because they had to have had help from the outside to plan their escape.

Of course, that help could have come from the inside. Other prisoners' contacts, security officers, chow hall staff, even counselors could be bought with money or sympathy.

For the life of him, he couldn't figure out why anyone would feel sorry for Robert Simpleton or the other two men because they'd committed heinous crimes against women.

The FBI was investigating the prison employees and inmates now. Even the warden had fallen under intense scrutiny.

Thankfully one of the prisoners Geoffrey Jones had been found. A Texas Ranger had beaten the feds to him and killed the bastard.

He chuckled. Sometimes the feds and Rangers fought over jurisdiction. But this time they'd welcomed the help. Dangerous prisoners on the loose tended to cause panic, and there had been four murders inside the prison in one month, meaning the FBI had their work cut out there.

Ranches and farmland sprawled across the terrain, reminding him of his own spread outside Austin. Lenora would need a safe place to hide until they caught Simpleton.

What would she think about going to his ranch with him?

An image of Lenora in his home taunted him. Lenora in his kitchen sipping coffee and sharing breakfast with him. Lenora outside riding across his land . . .

Jesus, he could not go there, could not start thinking about her in a personal way.

His job was to protect her and find Simpleton, not get involved with her.

Or fantasize about having her for himself.

No, detective work and relationships didn't mix.

He'd make sure Lenora was safe until Simpleton was back in the pen—or dead—then he'd leave her in peace again so she could find the happiness Simpleton had stolen from her.

LENORA ADJUSTED THE DISPLAY of wedding veils hanging by the floor length mirror, then moved on to straighten the shoe rack before rehanging the dresses Edie Nivens had spent the morning trying on.

Finally, the young bride-to-be had chosen a white strapless, sweetheart gown with lacy overlays. Lenora had taken her measurements for alterations and ordered shoes and the veil Edie had wanted.

Edie had left happy, relaxed and chattering nonstop about her upcoming big day.

A sliver of sadness threatened to destroy Lenora's good mood, but she tamped it down. Her mother and everyone else who'd known her before the attack thought she was crazy for opening a bridal shop when her own nuptials had been called off so suddenly.

When her heart had been broken.

But she'd rebelled against sympathy and the pitying stares—she'd endured too much of that after her abduction and the trial where she'd had to bare her soul in public.

So she'd chosen to dive into a career that would allow her to at least experience joy through others' happiness.

Just because she hadn't found true love and her happily-ever-after and didn't expect to, didn't mean that she couldn't enjoy helping others have that special day.

Truth was, the bridal shop had been cathartic for her. Too long she'd lived in that dark world, undergoing therapy, reliving the nightmares as she relayed details of her ordeal to lawyers and counselors, and then reading about her experiences in the paper the following day.

She had survived. But not without major scars, mostly invisible to others. The nightmares still tormented her at night. The demons and shadows still haunted her. The fear . . . threatened to immobilize her at the most unexpected times.

But she refused to succumb to that fear and let it paralyze her. Focusing on the darkness would rob her sanity.

And that would be a win for the sick bastard who'd hurt her.

Her assistant, Jenny Beal, flipped the closed sign on the front store door, then turned to her with a smile. "Whew. What a busy day."

"June is the big month for weddings." Which meant that brides-to-be had to order their dresses and start planning in the summer and fall. Rush jobs made everything more stressful and created unnecessary problems.

"Go on home," Lenora said. "I'll stay and finish for the day."

Jenny beamed a smile. "Thanks, Lenora. My boyfriend said he had plans for us tonight."

Lenora's heart fluttered. "You think he's going to propose?"

Jenny's green eyes lit up. "I don't know. I hope so!" She laughed, then practically bounced across the room in her excitement, her ponytail bobbing as she slung her purse over her shoulder and rushed out the back door.

Lenora watched her leave with a mixture of emotions. Joy for the twenty-three-year-old filled her. Even though she was only twenty-eight herself, she felt old. Ancient.

Hardened. Jaded.

And . . . lonely.

Had she ever been that naive and full of dreams?

Yes . . . before Robert Simpleton.

But he was locked away now and she was safe. That was all that mattered.

Sighing, she walked over to the cash register, tallied up the money and receipts for the day, then removed the credit card slips and checks and put them in the safe in her office. Tomorrow she'd make a bank deposit, but tonight she had a date with a bubble bath.

A noise sounded from the back, and she startled. Damn her nerves. It was probably just Jenny coming back for something. She was notorious for forgetting her keys.

She headed to the double doors leading to the back, but a knock on the front door made her jump.

Irritated with herself for being so jittery, she turned and walked to the front, then peered through the glass expecting to see Jenny.

But her breath caught at the sight of a man on the front stoop.

Not just any man. Sgt. Micah Hardin.

Memories flooded her. The dark prison room, his deep voice calling to her, his warm hand clasping hers and pulling her out, his strong arms carrying her to safety and into the light.

She'd had such a difficult time and hadn't trusted anyone but him back then, so the prosecutor had asked him to stay throughout the trial. His soft reassurances as he'd supported her through her testimony had saved her.

The familiar sting of tears, panic and fear seized her. She hadn't seen the Texas Ranger in years.

There was only one reason she could think of that he was here now.

Robert Simpleton must be out of jail.

And if he was, he was on his way to find her and kill her.

———————

MICAH'S GUT CLENCHED AT the instant fear that snapped into Lenora's eyes as she opened the door to her bridal shop.

Had she already heard about the prison escape?

Feminine scents suffused him as he stepped inside, the sight of dozens of bridal gowns, veils, shoes, and accessories striking him as ironic. He'd heard Lenora had opened a wedding shop and thought it odd since her fiancé had dumped her before the trial.

But an image of Lenora in the satin sheath hanging in front of the mirror to the right hit him, and his aching heart skipped a beat.

"Micah," she said in a throaty whisper. "You should have called."

"I wanted to see you in person." And offer my services to protect you.

She crossed her arms, her delicate jaw tightening just enough for him to see that she was nervous and trying to hide it. He'd noticed the same telltale signs at the trial.

Then he'd managed to soothe her because Simpleton was in custody.

Now . . .

"What happened?" she asked, her eyes searching his.

He wanted to lie and tell her that he'd just been in the area and thought he'd drop by and check on her. But he couldn't do that and protect her.

"Three prisoners broke out of the state pen," he said bluntly. "I'm afraid Robert Simpleton was one of them."

ROBERT SIMPLETON RIPPED OFF his prison uniform in the bathroom, grinning as he looked down at the initials he'd carved on his upper arm.

LL. Lenora Lockhart.

A vision of blond loveliness that had fueled his wet dreams in prison for the last few years. He wanted to touch her, hold her, shove his dick down her throat and inside her.

Make her pay for what she'd done to him.

All this time he'd done without a woman because of that bitch.

He yanked on the T-shirt and jeans his friend had stashed in the car for him, then pulled out the mustache and sideburns kit and began creating his disguise.

Lenora would remember the scraggly locks of hair that he once had, but she wouldn't recognize the shaved and totally tattooed head that was now his signature. The snakes that crawled across his bald head wrapped around a skeleton's bones.

Twenty minutes later, he eyed his new look in the mirror with a grin and admired the artwork that adorned his entire body.

Someone knocked on the door, then his friend's voice called his name.

"You about ready, Robert?"

He chuckled to himself. Keeping in good with Cissy had been a smart move on his part. Cissy had always wanted him.

He opened the door and hauled her inside. Her startled yelp turned to a sultry smile as he tore her shirt off, lowered his mouth and sucked her tits.

"God, Robert, I've wanted you for so long," she whispered.

She smelled like sweat, cigarettes, and booze, the latter two nearly making him gag. Lenora had smelled feminine, like lavender and sweetness, the way a woman should.

At least she had when he'd first abducted her.

Cissy ran her tongue across his jaw and anger sparked inside him. He didn't want her.

He wanted Lenora.

But Cissy ripped down his zipper and shoved at his pants, then closed her hand around his dick, and he groaned. If he didn't hurry, he was going to come all over her hand. He'd had enough hand jobs in prison.

Breath heaving, he spun her around, pushed her up against the bathroom wall, shoved her skirt up and gripped her hips. She wore black panties that he ripped with one hand, then he thrust his bulging cock inside her.

She groaned his name, clawing at the wall as he fucked her senseless. Their bodies slammed against each other, sweat sliding against sweat, his cock ramming harder and harder until he exploded inside her.

His cum dripped down her legs as he pulled out.

"I love you," she whispered. "Now we can finally be together."

Disgust filled him at the sight of her. Instead, Lenora's beautiful face flashed in his mind, taunting him.

Cissy might have wanted him forever. But he had other plans for his future.

A future that didn't involve her.

She twisted in his arms, smiling as she turned to face him, her tits red and swollen from his mouth, her eyes still glazed with passion.

And the promise of more.

But there would be no more for her. She'd served her purpose.

He slid one hand down and retrieved the pocketknife she'd included in the duffel bag, flipped it open and slit her throat.

Her gasp of pain and shock made his cock harden again, and he stroked himself as he watched the blood drain from her. Then he carefully carved the X between her breasts. He wanted to mark her as he had his other victims. Wanted the world to know that he was back.

Satisfied, he dropped her lifeless body to the floor, yanked his pants back up, grabbed the duffel bag, and stuffed the toiletry kit inside.

The clock was ticking, the minutes passing. The cops would be looking for him. They might warn Lenora he was coming.

But he'd find a way to get her.

To have her.

And this time no one would stop him.

CHAPTER 2

ICAH HATED THE PANIC that flickered across Lenora's face. But how could he blame her? He'd listened to every horrific detail of what Robert Simpleton had done to her and knew her mind was traveling back to that painful place.

A place he'd vowed she'd never have to visit again.

But if Simpleton found her, he would take her back there or worse. Who knew what kind of torture his sick mind had invented while he'd been locked in a cell?

Lenora leaned against a display of bridal books, her face paling. "How did it happen?"

"A fire broke out in the prison. While officers were moving inmates from that wing to another, one of the prisoners jumped an officer, stole his gun, and Simpleton and two other men escaped." Micah hesitated, wishing he had better news. "A statewide manhunt is underway, but at this point, we don't know where Simpleton is."

"He'll come after me," Lenora said in a matter-of-fact voice.

He wanted to argue that fact, but there was no use. She had lived with the man for three weeks—she knew his evil, sadistic side. Worse, they'd both heard him promise retribution for her testimony at the sentencing.

Simpleton was a cold-blooded murderer. Lenora was the only victim who'd survived.

The one who'd put him in jail.

He wouldn't stop until he exacted his revenge.

LENORA GRIPPED THE EDGE of the table to steady herself. She could not fall apart in front of Micah.

He'd witnessed her weak side, seen her at her worst. But she'd worked too hard to overcome her fears and nightmares to allow herself to backtrack.

But how could she not?

Robert Simpleton was conniving, smart, a sociopath—and there was no doubt that he wanted revenge against her. It wasn't if he would show up, but *when*.

She had to be prepared.

The self-defense classes she'd taken hopefully would help, although at the moment, every move and technique she'd been taught escaped her.

Because the old familiar panic was back, gnawing at her insides like a rabid animal.

"You should probably shut down the shop for a few days, or at least take off until we catch Simpleton," Micah said. "Do you want me to drive you some place? Maybe to your mother's?"

Lenora's head was spinning, the instinct to run hitting her. "Not my mother's," she said. "I won't do anything to put her in jeopardy."

Micah's dark brown eyes pierced her. "Is there a friend or other family member you can stay with? Some place Simpleton might not know about?"

"No." Her withdrawal and depression after the abduction had cost her all of her former friends. She and Jenny were close now but on a working basis.

Even her relationship with her mother had become strained. Her mother wanted to protect her, wanted her to live at home with her. But Lenora had to regain her independence or she'd go insane.

Still, Simpleton wouldn't know that. He was a monster who preyed on women. He'd use Jenny, even her mother to get to her.

"If he doesn't already know about my bridal shop, it'll be easy for him to find out," Lenora said, forcing herself to think defensively. "If I can't convince my mother and friend Jenny to go away, I want protection for them."

"Done." He removed his phone from his belt. "Why don't you call them and explain while I talk to my superior."

Lenora nodded, moving on rote. Jenny was a sweetheart and a great employee. She was also one of the only friends she'd made since her ordeal.

One who didn't know about her past.

Lenora needed her privacy, needed someone who wouldn't look at her with pity.

She clenched her hands into fists. God, she hated to dirty Jenny with the details now.

But if Robert Simpleton hurt Jenny or her mother, she'd never forgive herself.

Her phone buzzed, and she glanced down, not surprised to see her mother's number. She must have seen the news and would be terrified. She'd handle her, then her friend.

But she had to tell Jenny in person, convince her that Simpleton was dangerous.

Her hands itched to retrieve the gun she'd bought after the attack. She'd vowed never to be as vulnerable as she had been the night he'd taken her. Never to let down her guard.

When that monster came for her, she had to be ready. And if he tried to touch her, she'd blown his brains out.

———————

MICAH STEPPED OUTSIDE THE shop to make the phone call, carefully keeping an eye on the street and doorway in case Simpleton showed up. Odds were that the man already knew where Lenora lived and worked.

And that he'd come in disguise.

Photographs of him were plastered all over the news and papers. He'd have to alter his appearance.

The bridal shop sat on the corner of one street next to a florist and bakery that probably made it easier for Lenora's clients and her to coordinate their events.

He punched in the number to contact his superior, Lieutenant Angus Roper, while visually assessing the area surrounding Lenora's shop as the phone began to ring. Being on the corner meant no neighbors on one side, allowing access from the front, a side window, and the back.

A street separated the building from the next row of businesses which housed a beauty parlor, barber shop, tack shop and boot store. Midday, cars filled most of the spaces along the streets, and a dozen were parked in a lot beside the diner. People were going in and out of businesses, mothers strolling babies along the sidewalk, a florist delivery man loading the back of his van with flowers.

The phone buzzed twice while he walked to the corner then to the side and back. An alley ran along the back of the buildings with parking for employees, dumpsters, and loading docks for vendors.

His stomach knotted as he searched for security cameras and found none.

The phone buzzed again, then Lt. Roper's throaty voice echoed back. "Where are you, Hardin?"

"Outside Lenora Lockhart's Bridal Shop."

"How'd she take the news?"

"As well as can be expected. She's worried about her mother and coworker, afraid Simpleton will try to use one of them to get to her."

"She's probably right."

"She's going to warn them. If they can't stay with a friend or leave town, I want to assign them protection in case Simpleton shows up."

"Good idea. If he does, maybe we can catch him and put the bastard back in jail where he belongs."

"Do we have any idea who helped him?"

"We might have a lead. We've been studying the visitor logs for the escaped inmates. Some hairdresser named Cissy Cornwell used to visit Simpleton. She might have been helping him."

Micah glanced at the beauty parlor, wondering if she'd set up shop there to spy on Lenora. "Did she know him before he was locked up?"

"No, she met him when she visited her brother in the pen. They started writing, and she became his sole visitor."

"Must have her own sadistic side to fall for a man who brutalized women the way Simpleton did."

"There are a lot of nutcases out there."

"I'll check her out." He copied down her address, hoping Cissy might give them information to help find Simpleton.

"We're interviewing other inmates and the feds have Simpleton's cellmate in interrogation. I'll let you know what we learn."

Micah hung up, images of Simpleton's other victims flashing back. Then an image of Lenora the day he'd rescued her. Lenora, beaten and bruised, dehydrated, dirty, traumatized and covered in filth.

Locking Simpleton up had been one of the best days of his life.

This time, he might not bother with jail. He'd put the bastard in the ground.

LENORA GRITTED HER TEETH as she answered her mother's phone call. "Mom, I was getting ready to call you."

"Then you know that monster escaped from prison. It's been all over the news." Terror streaked her mother's shrill voice.

"Yes, Sgt. Hardin is here with me now."

"Ask him how in the hell he let this happen."

"Mother," Lenora said, injecting a calmness to her voice when she felt like screaming at the situation herself. "It's not his fault," she said instead. "The police have a statewide manhunt underway now. They'll find him."

Her mother made a sarcastic sound. "But he never should have escaped. And what if he finds you?" She exhaled a shaky breath. "He threatened you in court. He's probably on his way—"

"You don't need to remind me." Lenora's voice took on a razor edge as painful memories assaulted her. She could feel the oppressive darkness closing around her. Smell the scent of his sweaty body. Sensed his breath on her neck.

"Pack your bags and stay with me until he's caught," her mother said. "I'll hire a bodyguard for you."

"No," Lenora said emphatically. God help her. She appreciated the fact that her mother had taken care of her after she was released from the hospital, but her hovering and worrying and constant crying had only made things worse. Lenora found herself comforting her mother and trying to assure her that her captivity hadn't been that bad, but it had been. And neither of them could change it.

Only therapy and time had helped her heal and quieted the nightmares.

"I appreciate your offer, Mom, but Sgt. Hardin is here now. I want you to stay with a friend, or maybe have Aunt Gladys stay with you until Simpleton is caught."

A tense heartbeat passed. "You think he'll come to me?"

"I don't know, Mother, but we can't take any chances. Will you do that for me?"

Her mother sighed. "Yes, but only if you promise that you have protection." Her mother's voice cracked. "I don't want that psycho to hurt you again. You're all I have left, Lenora."

Emotions welled in Lenora's throat. "I promise, Mom."

"All right," her mother said. "Please be careful, sweetheart."

"You, too." Lenora wiped at a tear as she ended the call.

Micah stepped back inside, his eyes searching hers. "Are you okay?"

A nervous laugh bubbled in her throat. "No. But I will be."

His eyes twinkled with something akin to admiration. Or maybe she'd imagined it because a second later it was gone.

"I want to warn Jenny in person."

His gaze met hers. "Does she know about Simpleton?"

She shook her head, wondering if that was censure in his eyes. "I hashed everything over enough in court and therapy. I wanted her to respect me, not look at me with pity or like I was too fragile to handle a business."

"I respect you, Lenora," Micah said softly. "It took guts to stand up to that psychopath and testify."

Lenora's heart fluttered. Micah had known her during the

most difficult time of her life. She'd wondered what he thought about her, had even thought that if they'd met under different circumstances there could have been more between them.

But Robert Simpleton had ruined her future with any man.

"Thank you for saying that, Sergeant."

"Micah." He shifted as if he wanted to say something else then cleared his throat. "We may have a lead on a woman who visited Simpleton in prison." He gestured toward the door. "If you want to lock up, I'll drive you to see your friend and you can stay with her while I pay her a visit."

"I can't stay with Jenny. It would be too dangerous for her."

"Then you'll go with me. I'm not leaving you alone until he's caught."

Lenora moved on autopilot, straightening the store and closing up, well aware of Micah's presence. His big body seemed to occupy all the air in the room, but not the way Robert Simpleton's had. The very memory of the man's filthy hands on her made nausea churn in her belly.

Micah's masculine scent evoked a sense of safety as if he would protect her no matter what.

And those dark eyes of his stirred a longing that she'd never thought she'd feel again.

MICAH'S CHEST POUNDED WITH the effort it took him not to pull Lenora up against him and comfort her. He knew every vile thing the man had done to her, had seen her brutalized body when he'd rescued her. And the images of the crime photos were forever imprinted in his brain.

He would not let Simpleton touch her again.

But an odd tingling had started in his body when she'd looked into his eyes. She looked vulnerable, but . . . tough. Determined to survive.

Just as she had at the trial. She had survived because she was strong and had used her wits with Simpleton.

She'd even tried to save the other two women who'd been held captive with her, had offered to trade her life for theirs.

Unfortunately, Simpleton had gotten off on her spunk and had punished her by making her watch him torture them.

ROBERT STUFFED THE CASH Cissy had given him into his duffel bag, then searched her house for the secret stash she'd confessed she kept for emergencies. Five thousand. Not a lot, but enough for food and a cheap motel for the night. He needed to lay low, stay off the grid.

Keep hidden until he found the perfect place to take Lenora. He'd look for it tomorrow. Another house just like the one he'd grown up in.

But first things first.

His pattern was threes. Even the stupid cunt reporter Jamie Thornton had picked up on that. She'd dubbed him with that ridiculous name, the Trio Killer, which was pathetic compared to some of the famous serial killers in history.

At least she could have given him a respectable title like the Hunter or Casanova or the Heartbreaker.

Except he didn't really break his victims' hearts. He just drove a knife into them.

Laughter gurgled in his throat as he lifted the lid off the shoebox in Cissy's closet and dug out the cash. Her vibrator lay inside as if it was a prized possession she had to take with her in case of a hasty escape.

Damn dildo was puny compared to him. Yes, Cissy had liked his giant cock. So had the other women.

Well, maybe some of them wouldn't admit it, but all whores liked it rough. Hell, they'd deserved what he'd done to them. They'd screamed in pain when he rammed it inside them as if their delicate little chambers were too fragile to fuck him.

He'd shown them.

He was in control.

He tossed the shoebox and dildo back in the closet, grabbed the beer Cissy had stored in the frig for him and hurried out the back door. A second later, he was cruising down the road in the old pickup Cissy had bought for him. With a chaw of tobacco in his mouth, a cowboy hat and the jeans and shirt she'd bought for him, he looked like any other cowboy in Texas, not an escaped felon on the run.

Yes, little Cissy had been so helpful. She'd done everything he'd told her to do. Followed his orders to the T. Made sure she used cash to buy the truck so no one could trace him through it.

The temptation to press the accelerator hit him. He'd been penned up so damn long he wanted to roll down the window and feel the warm Texas air blowing in his face as he flew down the highway. He flipped on the radio to a good country station and began to belt along with Johnny Cash.

But a siren wailed in the distance, reminding him that he was a wanted man, and he slowed, then veered onto a side road. The cops couldn't be everywhere. They'd be putting up roadblocks on major highways, checking airports, bus and train stations. But no way they had enough manpower to cover all the offbeat little roads that wove through the countryside.

He simply had to focus on not drawing attention to himself.

And decide whom he was going to snatch first before he went after Lenora. It had to be someone she knew. Someone she wouldn't want to suffer.

Someone she'd let him do anything he wanted to do to her in order to save them.

He had a list he'd compiled in prison. He tapped his fingers on the steering column to *Walk the Line*, laughing as he tried to decide which woman to take first.

CHAPTER 3

MICAH PLUGGED CISSY CORNWELL's address into his phone to get directions while Lenora ducked into a back room and grabbed her purse. Once he had the address, he phoned the beauty parlor down the street on the off chance that Cissy was there.

A female answered. "Susie Jo's Salon."

"I'm looking for Cissy Cornwall. Is she working today?"

A hesitation. "No, she only worked here for a couple of weeks. Got her paycheck then disappeared on us."

Just enough time to stalk Lenora and tell her boyfriend where she was. "You haven't spoken to her this week?"

"No, and I tried her cell, but her phone was disconnected."

Figured. "Okay, thanks."

He ended the call just as Lenora returned. "I'm ready."

"Why don't I follow you home, then we can drop your car, and I'll drive you to your friend's."

She nodded, her expression grim as she headed to the door. He stood by her side, eyeing the outside of the shop and the street as she locked the door, although he couldn't help but notice her hands were trembling, and she almost dropped the keys twice.

"Sorry," she said with a wary smile.

He couldn't help himself. He gently touched her elbow, aching to do something to assuage her pain. "You have nothing to be sorry for, Lenora. You have good reason to be nervous. But I'm here, and I'll do everything in my power to keep you safe."

Emotions flickered in her eyes as she looked up at him. "I won't let him break me," she said with a stubborn tilt to her chin.

Admiration for her made his chest squeeze. "I know, but you're not alone. This time we know he's coming. We'll be ready."

She studied him for a moment, anguish in her eyes. No doubt she was reliving the night of the abduction. Simpleton had stalked her for weeks. Learned her routine. Gone through her garbage. Even known her time of the month.

He'd cleverly watched her leave her aerobics class and snatched her when she'd reached her car. She had no idea what had happened until she'd regained consciousness in that cell of a room where he'd kept her.

Micah followed her to her car, a red Toyota, not surprised that she'd changed vehicles. Blood from where she'd scratched at Simpleton during the attack had been found on the driver's side of her Honda Civic.

And then there had been her blood.

She climbed in, and he got in his SUV and followed her as she maneuvered the small town and turned into a gated townhome complex that looked modern and impersonal, not the kind of place where he pictured Lenora. She paused at the gate to input a security code, making him feel marginally better about the location and the fact that at least she lived in a secure neighborhood.

She parked in an assigned spot in front of a two-story stucco unit then slid from the driver's seat.

"Do you like it here?" he asked as she slipped into his SUV.

She shrugged. "I wanted some place with people around. The floor plan offers space, but the second-floor terrace is where I spend a lot of time."

He nodded, remembering her statement after the attack about not being able to breathe. That she wanted open spaces, not to feel confined. Somehow, he pictured her on a ranch, *his* ranch, with acres of land to roam, plush pastures, ponds, and creeks.

"You have a view?"

"From the terrace, you can see the town and the canyon. At night it's beautiful."

So was she.

But he bit his tongue, wondering what in the hell was wrong with him. He'd never been attracted to a witness or victim before.

Why couldn't he get her out of his mind?

———————

LENORA TEXTED JENNY THAT she had to talk to her and that she was on her way. Jenny promised to wait.

Lenora gave Micah directions, grateful he didn't push her for conversation. She was struggling to keep her emotions at bay and silently willing herself not to fall apart. Micah would protect her. Police were looking for Robert Simpleton. They would find him.

Shuddering at the memory of that knife at her throat while he forced himself on her, she blinked to stem the tears. Micah reached across the console and laid his hand over hers. A gentle squeeze. A tender touch.

It was almost enough to make her come undone.

After the attack, she'd handled the press, the questions, even the brutal way Simpleton's attorney had questioned her. Had she seduced Simpleton? Had they met before? Maybe she'd come on to him and given him the wrong idea.

She'd even tolerated the curious stares and horrified looks of those who'd heard her story.

But the simple kind touches nearly brought her to her knees.

She spotted Jenny's bungalow at the dead end of the street and pointed it out to Micah. "There. That's Jenny's with the bird sanctuary."

Micah steered the SUV into the drive and cut the engine, then climbed out and started around to her side. Lenora opened the door, deciding she couldn't lean on him too much.

That might get to be a habit. Then what would she do when he left?

She needed her independence. She'd worked too hard to regain it to relinquish it now.

A muscle ticked in his jaw as they walked up to the front door. Jenny had planted a flower garden to the right, the flowers dancing in the evening breeze, orange and yellow against the green grass. The sun had set, the rainbow of colors majestic on the horizon, reminding her how beautiful Texas was.

Yet there was nothing beautiful about what she'd come to do. She would be exposing her worst pain, her biggest humiliation. Bringing her new friend into the dark world, she'd barely survived.

Damn Robert Simpleton. She hated him more than she'd ever thought possible to hate another living soul.

Micah knocked, and a second later Jenny answered, a handsome blond guy beside her dressed in jeans, a dressy western shirt, and boots. Lenora had met him once; his name was Troy Benson. Jenny was totally in love, and Lenora could see the adoration on Troy's face as he threw an arm around Jenny.

But a worried look pulled at Jenny's heart-shaped face as she glanced at Micah. "Come on in, Lenora. What's going on?"

Lenora gestured toward Micah. "This is Sgt. Micah Hardin with the Texas Rangers."

Jenny introduced her boyfriend then led them to the den. Light colors and lots of throw pillows and rugs gave it a classy but comfortable feel.

Lenora folded her hands in her lap, twisting her fingers. "There's something I have to tell you." She exhaled a deep breath. "Something I should have told you a long time ago."

Jenny's eyes clouded over. "He escaped, didn't he?"

Lenora swallowed hard. "What?"

"The man who kidnapped you and . . . hurt you," Jenny said softly. "I saw the news. He escaped from prison."

Lenora was too stunned to speak for a moment. "You knew? How? When?" Lenora gulped. "Why didn't you say anything?"

Jenny's expression softened. "I figured you'd tell me when you were ready."

Jenny opened her arms and wrapped them around Lenora. Lenora choked on a sob, desperately trying to hold herself together. Footsteps shuffled, and she realized Micah and Troy had discreetly left the room to give them some privacy.

"I'm sorry, Jenny," Lenora said, swiping at her tears. "It's just been so . . . hard."

"I hope they kill the maniac," Jenny said, her voice fierce.

Lenora laughed through her tears. "Me, too." She pulled away and clenched Jenny's hands. Maybe while she'd been hiding out here, trying not to get close to anyone, trying to shield herself, she'd actually found a new best friend.

"So, YOU THINK THIS creep is coming after Lenora?" Troy asked.

Micah nodded. "Oh, yeah. He wants revenge."

Troy raked a hand through his thick hair, sending the ends standing up. "So why did Lenora come to see Jenny? Is Lenora going to disappear until he's caught?"

"If I have anything to do with it, yes," Micah said, knowing Lenora would probably balk. "But Simpleton might use anyone Lenora cares about to trap her."

Troy's blue eyes narrowed to angry slits. "You mean he might try to kidnap Jenny?"

"That's exactly what I mean," Micah said.

Troy leaned against the kitchen counter, his arms crossed. "He'll have to kill me first."

If the situation hadn't been so grave, and if he didn't know how sadistic Simpleton was, Micah would have almost smiled at Troy's protective stance. "My advice would be to take Jenny somewhere safe."

"What about the business?" Troy asked. "Jenny and Lenora will never leave their clients in a bind."

Micah sighed. He was afraid that would be a problem. "Is there anyone who can cover the shop for a few days?"

Troy shrugged. "They have a lady named Wilma who answers the phones and mans the business when they go out on consults. I think she's been on vacation the last couple of weeks, but she just got back."

"I'll talk to Lenora," Micah said. "Maybe they can leave her in charge. I can always put a guard at the shop in case Simpleton shows up there."

"We can't do that." Lenora's voice cut into the room, and Micah glanced up and saw her and Jenny standing side by side as if they'd already planned their strategy.

Micah had a bad feeling he wasn't going to like it.

LENORA HAD TO STAND her ground. "I know what you're going to suggest, but he wants me, Micah. If I hide, he'll only hurt others until he can have me."

"He may do that anyway," Micah said. "So you're sure as hell not going to offer yourself as bait."

"I'm not talking about that," Lenora said. "But we have a big wedding in a couple of weeks. I can't just leave my client in a bind." Because when this was over, her business might be the only thing she had left.

His jaw tightened, his features rigid with anger. And something else she couldn't quite define.

"I want you out of here," Troy said to Jenny.

"Troy—"

"I read about the things he did to those women," Troy said, his tone harsh. Then, as if he realized Lenora had been one of those women, he gave her a contrite look. "I'm sorry, Lenora. I just don't want Jenny hurt."

"Neither do I," Lenora said, battling a wave of emotions crowding her chest. Sucking in a breath of courage, she turned to her friend. "Jenny, please leave town with Troy. We'll stay in touch, and I'll call you as soon as they find Simpleton."

Jenny shook her head. "I want to be here and help you, Lenora."

Lenora gripped her friend's hands. "You will help me by easing my mind. Please, Jenny. I know what this man is capable of." She swallowed revulsion at the memories tearing at her mind. "I couldn't live with myself if he hurt you."

Troy wrapped a possessive arm around Jenny's shoulder. "Don't worry. No one is going to hurt my sweetheart."

"But—"

"No argument." Troy's eyes heated with the kind of love and lust that Lenora had read about only in books. "I've been wanting a little time away with you. Now's we can have it."

Jenny looked reluctant, but Troy kissed her, and she finally agreed.

Lenora's heart pounded with relief. At least if Jenny stayed with Troy, she'd be safe.

MICAH WAS GRATEFUL HE and Troy had won that battle, and the women decided to let Wilma handle the shop, but he was still worried about Lenora. He wanted to whisk her away and make sure Simpleton couldn't find her.

He wanted to hold her and kiss her.

Idiot. He absolutely could not do the latter.

Why was she getting to him so badly? He'd been assigned to protect other women before; witnesses to crimes, women in danger from stalkers. But none of them had wormed their way into his head, and his heart, like she had.

"Where does the woman who helped Simpleton live?" Lenora asked as he shifted into gear and pulled away from Jenny's house.

"An apartment in Austin."

"Did she know Simpleton before he was incarcerated?"

"No. She met him in prison when she was visiting her brother." Hell, maybe they'd luck up and find Simpleton with her. Then he could lock his sorry ass back up where it belonged.

Or kill him if Simpleton resisted.

He *hoped* the bastard resisted.

After all, Simpleton had escaped once. He could escape again. The only way Lenora would be truly safe was if the monster was dead.

"Apparently she was a hairdresser. She worked at the beauty shop down the street for a couple of weeks."

Lenora gasped. "She was stalking me so she could report to Simpleton?"

"It appears that way."

Lenora lapsed into silence as he drove, the tension between them palpable. The city lights of Austin gleamed ahead, and Micah could almost hear the country music blaring from the bars.

His GPS indicated for him to turn on to a side street before they reached the city limits. The dry Texas land had taken a hit with drought, the heat and lack of rain causing the cedar trees to die, making the land look barren in the moonlight.

The apartment complex looked old and dated, the scraggly bushes in front in desperate need of manicuring, the stucco dirty and fading. Another car pulled in, its lights flashing bright against the cement.

Unlike Lenora's upscale complex, this one had no security gate.

Lenora shuddered. "I don't understand women who fall for prisoners, especially a cruel man like Simpleton."

"Psychopaths can be quite charming when they want," Micah said wryly.

He noted the building numbers, then spotted 3A, Cissy's apartment, and parked in front beside a dirty white sedan. The streetlight was broken, making the parking lot look shadowy, almost eerie with the empty spaces.

When he cut the engine, he turned to Lenora.

"Do you want to wait here?"

She shook her head no. "If he's here, I want to watch you arrest him. And if he's not, I need to talk to this woman."

Not that it would do any good, Micah thought. He'd heard stories about women who fell for inmates. They thought they could save them or some bullshit like that.

But he was determined to make this as easy on Lenora as possible. If confronting Simpleton or his accomplice would help her in any way, he'd do it.

He squeezed her hand. "Just stay behind me and take my lead. Simpleton might be armed."

She nodded, opened her car door and slid out. He did the same, one hand stroking the gun at his hip as they neared the door. Weeds choked the few feet of grass; the front stoop was streaked with stains. The door looked like pressed wood and was starting to rot.

He knocked on the door, stepping forward so that Lenora stood behind him. They waited several seconds, but no one answered. He knocked again, then leaned his ear against the door, listening for sounds someone was inside.

"She's not here," Lenora said. Disappointment tinged her voice.

He held up a finger to quiet her, then turned the doorknob. The door screeched open. Micah pulled his gun and aimed it at the ready as he slowly inched inside.

"Texas Ranger, Miss Cornwell. If you're in here, please answer."

His voice echoed back as if the place was empty. Ratty, out-dated furniture was cluttered with laundry, beauty magazines, and fast food wrappers.

"Miss Cornwell?"

He felt Lenora close on his heels and pressed a hand to hers to urge her to stay behind him as he inched deeper inside the room. A faint beam of moonlight glimmered through the sheer, worn curtains giving him enough light to see a room to the right.

He slowly approached it and peered inside. An unmade bed, the sheets tousled. A chair holding a pile of women's clothes. Makeup bottles and brushes scattered across an ancient dresser.

The hair on the back of his neck prickled as an acrid odor hit him. Blood . . . death.

"Wait," he whispered to Lenora.

He moved forward, hand gripping his gun, then pushed open the bathroom door. His stomach knotted at the sight in front of him.

Cissy Cornwell was lying on the bathroom floor, her eyes gaping in the shock of death, blood soaking her neck and chest.

CHAPTER 4

L ENORA GASPED, A DEEP trembling starting inside her that made her cold all over. Cissy Cornwell lay in a pool of her own blood, her lips parted, one bloody hand reaching out as if to plead for her lover to save her.

Simpleton had probably enjoyed watching her beg for her life, seeing the shock on her face, the realization that she'd risked everything to help him. Yet in the end, he'd made her suffer just as he had his other victims.

"Son of a bitch," Micah muttered.

"He used her, then killed her," she said, her voice thick.

"Yeah, and now she can't tell us anything." Micah knelt to examine her body, although it was obvious she was dead. She'd lost a lot of blood, her complexion was pasty, her eyes glazed.

"Body's just starting to go into rigor," Micah said. "That means Simpleton can't be too far away."

Lenora glanced around the bathroom in search of signs of Simpleton. Women's toiletries. Cheap perfume. Fake eyelashes. Peroxide for her hair.

Or was it for Simpleton's? He could have dyed it white.

Another scan of the small bathroom and she noticed wrappers from a kit, mustache and sideburns. He'd obviously donned a disguise.

What did he look like now?

Micah pulled his phone from his pocket and made a call. "Yes, Lieutenant, this is Hardin. I'm at Cissy Cornwell's apartment. She's dead." A hesitation. "Yes, it was him. He slashed her throat."

Although he'd stabbed his other victims in the heart. Why hadn't he done so with Cissy?

Lenora's eyes were drawn to the bloody X on the woman's chest, and she started to shake uncontrollably. The bloody X was just like the one he'd carved on all his victims, including her.

After the crime scene photographs had been taken at the hole where she'd been kept and then again at the hospital, the nurse had washed away the bloody X. Except Simpleton had carved it deep enough to leave a scar. A plastic surgeon had taken care of it soon afterward.

But in her mind, it would always be there.

A permanent reminder of what he'd done to her.

In the early stages after her release, when she'd suffered severe panic attacks and nightmares, she'd wake up screaming that she had to get rid of that damned X. She'd scrubbed her skin raw trying to erase it. The doctor assured her it wasn't visible.

But she saw it every time she looked in the mirror.

"Send a crime unit," Micah said. "And see if you can find out what kind of car she drove. Maybe Simpleton's in it now."

Lenora's heart raced. Could it be that simple? They'd locate the make and model, issue an APB and the police would catch him.

A shiver tore through her. No. Robert Simpleton was a cunning planner. He hadn't escaped on a whim. He'd carefully orchestrated his escape just as he had his abductions.

Which meant he probably already had a list of his next victims. She was top on that list. But who else would he take?

A random woman or someone connected to her?

MICAH WISHED TO HELL that Lenora wasn't with him. He hated that she'd seen Cissy's dead body and knew that the bloody X on the woman's chest triggered painful memories.

"Lenora, once the crime unit arrives, I'll take you home."

Her eyes flared with determination. "No, do what you need to do to find him." She pointed to the trash and the wrappers. "It looks like he may have altered his appearance."

Micah nodded. "In prison, they cut his hair. Our computer team can run his picture through our program to show how he might look in different disguises, with different hair and facial hair. Then we'll show it on the news."

Lenora wiped perspiration from her forehead. "Did he leave the knife he used to kill her?"

Micah scanned the small bathroom. "I don't see it anywhere.

He probably took it with him."

"To use again," Lenora said through clenched teeth.

Micah couldn't argue with that point. He used his phone to capture several photographs of Cissy's body, focusing on details of the way she was lying, the blood pools, and her clothing which was strewn across the bathroom.

He looked in the trash and saw Simpleton's prison jumpsuit and photographed it as well. "He didn't even try to cover his tracks."

Lenora grimaced. "He wants me to know he's coming."

Micah gripped her arms. "Look at me, Lenora. He may come after you, but I won't let him hurt you again. I promise."

Lenora's lower lip quivered. "Don't make promises you can't keep, Micah."

She was right. But he had to make her feel safe.

"I will keep this one," he said softly.

Her gaze met his, emotions darkening her eyes. She wanted to trust him; that was obvious. But she also understood the kind of monster they were dealing with, and if Simpleton found a way to get Micah out of the way, he might trap Lenora again.

He couldn't let that happen. He had to stay focused.

He dropped his hands and took a step away, needing the distance. Becoming personally entangled with Lenora would only cloud his judgment.

"I'm going to look around, see if I can find any sign where Simpleton was headed."

"Probably to find another victim. You know he always takes three women."

"Yes, but I'm not sure Cissy counts. The MO is different."

"Because he knew her," Lenora said.

"Maybe. She might be different to him because she actually did love him."

Lenora's stomach rolled. "You're right. He tried to force us to say that we loved him. But when the other women did, he grew enraged, called them liars and killed them."

"Cissy was a means to an end, not part of his sick demented MO. He wanted to get rid of her quick and fast."

Lenora inhaled a deep breath. "Tell me what to do, and I'll help."

He removed two pairs of latex gloves from his pocket, tossed one to her, then yanked on the other pair. "Look for her purse while I search the desk and kitchen. If you find something, let me know, and we'll bag and tag it to send to the lab. But be sure to put everything else back where you find it."

Lenora nodded, pulled on the gloves then ducked into the closet in search of the purse. Seconds later, she came out empty handed. "Judging from the unopened boxes in the closet, Cissy had an addiction to the shopping channel. But her purse isn't in there."

"Check the den and kitchen."

She disappeared into the other room while he strode over to the small desk in the bedroom corner. No computer or cell phone. A quick scan through the drawers turned up nothing but unpaid bills and a dry cleaning stub.

"I found her purse," she called.

"Is there a cell phone in it?"

"No."

Dammit, Simpleton probably took it. Although he'd be too smart to use it. Because he knew they'd check Cissy's caller ID log and text history. Was there something on there he didn't want them to see?

He'd ask forensics to pull her phone records and examine them.

"Go through her purse," Micah said as he stepped into the den. "Look for an address book, notes, anything that might give us a clue where he's going. The name of a motel, another friend who might be helping."

"I'm looking."

Micah opened the refrigerator and found a cheap bottle of wine and two steaks. Cissy had obviously planned a celebratory romantic dinner, but Simpleton had had other plans. He spotted a grocery receipt on the counter and skimmed it. Ahh, she'd also bought beer which Simpleton obviously had taken.

He closed the refrigerator, then looked inside the cabinets and found tacky orange flowered dishes that looked like they'd come from a yard sale along with mismatched chipped coffee mugs.

A basket on the counter held junk mail and unpaid bills. He thumbed through them, deciding Cissy must have been a hairbreadth away from being evicted. A convenience store receipt confirmed that she'd bought two burner phones, so she'd probably given one to Simpleton to take with him.

Then he hit pay dirt. He found a receipt for a pickup truck and a tag, both paid for in cash.

A siren wailed, and he realized it was probably the crime unit so he told Lenora he'd be back, then stepped outside the apartment to meet them. His phone was ringing, so he swiped to answer it.

"Hardin, it's Lt. Roper. We found out what kind of car Cissy Cornwell owned. A white Toyota sedan."

"It's in the parking lot," Micah said. "But I found a receipt for a black pickup truck. My guess is that's what Simpleton's driving."

"Give me the details, and I'll issue an APB."

Micah recited the license number, well aware that Simpleton might remove or disguise the tag, but hoping that the make and model would be enough to catch the police's attention on the road.

It would be a miracle if they caught the asshole before he killed again.

He just wished he believed in miracles.

LENORA FELT AS IF she was violating Cissy's privacy by searching through her purse, a cheap vinyl, oversized orange bag that was packed with junk. Yet the woman had helped a cruel madman escape prison so he could wreak havoc again on innocent women's lives.

Had Cissy not understood how brutal and violent the man was? Hadn't she read the papers and seen the list of his victims?

If so, how could she possibly have aided in his escape?

She pulled out a comb, hairspray, and perfume along with a red wallet. She opened it and glanced at Cissy's driver's license.

The woman was only twenty-nine, but the cigarettes she found inside explained why she looked older and the reason for her yellowed teeth. Two lighters and matches from a bar that sounded vaguely like a strip joint were at the bottom of the bag.

Micah had said Cissy was a hairdresser, but she could have moonlighted as a waitress, stripper or . . . prostitute.

She laid each of the items she removed on the coffee table. A fire engine red lipstick. Compact. Make up bag with eyeliner, blue eyeshadow and enough rouge to paint a clown's face.

Next, she discovered a stack of envelopes wrapped in a rubber band. She pulled them out, expecting to see bills, but when she looked at the return address, she realized they were from the state prison.

Her stomach churned as she opened the first one and began to read.

> *Dear Cissy,*
>
> *I am so grateful to find you, my love. You are such a special woman. Each night as I lie on my cot, I think of how beautiful you are, how delicate your face is. How tender and soft your skin will feel when I finally touch it.*
>
> *I dream about you every night now. Dream of the two of us kissing and holding each other. Of long walks in the moonlight. Of long nights where we make love and hold each other until dawn.*
>
> *Seeing you is like seeing the sunshine that I miss so much. I can't wait until I'm free and we're together.*
> *Love always,*
> *Robbie*

Lenora's hand shook as she dropped the letter. Her pulse pounded as she opened another one and read it. More of the same. Loving words and promises, tender thoughts and dreams of gentle touches, memories Simpleton proclaimed to want to make with Cissy. Even love poems he'd carefully copied in some kind of script writing that looked elegant and lovely.

Not at all like the ugly monster beneath that façade.

With each letter, Lenora grew increasingly angry. Simpleton had completely conned Cissy into believing he'd been victimized, that she'd told lies about him, that he'd been falsely imprisoned.

Then Cissy had helped him and gotten her throat slit for doing so.

The bastard deserved to die.

She wanted to rip the letters into a million pieces and burn them, but common sense reminded her they were evidence.

And that she was supposed to be looking for something to help them track down Simpleton.

She carefully placed the letters back in their envelopes for the crime team, then dug in the purse once again and found a small black book. She opened it and skimmed the pages, but all the names listed were men.

Clients? Not from a hair salon . . .

Had Simpleton known she was a hooker on the side? If he hadn't and he'd discovered it when he escaped, it might have triggered his rage.

Not that she believed that the man had loved Cissy. No . . . he was incapable of love.

He had coldly used Cissy then discarded her just as he did all the women in his life.

———————

MICAH FILLED THE CRIME unit in on what he suspected had happened, then led them inside Cissy's apartment.

"I've looked for a computer and cell phone but didn't find one. Simpleton left his prison uniform in the trash, but we need to process it for forensics just to confirm it was his."

"Did you find the weapon?"

"No." Micah gritted his teeth as Lenora looked up at him from the couch. Her expression looked tormented, but he decided not to question her until they were alone. After all, technically she shouldn't have been handling evidence.

One of the techs collected the purse from Lenora.

"He snowed Cissy with love letters," she said in a whisper so only Micah could hear.

"He's a sociopath," Micah murmured. "He changes faces like a chameleon."

Lenora nodded and crossed her arms, and Micah turned back to the CSI team.

"The body is in the bathroom." The ME appeared, and Micah led the way.

"She's been dead only a few hours," he said. "We haven't found a computer or cell. Pull her phone records and let me know what you find."

The ME knelt to examine her. "You're right. Body's still slightly warm."

He didn't need the doctor to tell him cause of death. She'd bled out within minutes from the knife wound.

"I'm going to drive Lenora home," he said. "Look for something that might indicate where Simpleton's going next."

The CSI nodded, and Micah stepped back into the den. "Come on, Lenora. Let's go back to your place."

She followed him outside to his SUV, unusually quiet.

"I'm sorry you had to see that," he said softly as they settled inside.

"I saw him kill before," she said as if the sight of Cissy's dead body hadn't bothered her.

"I know," he said. "But that's supposed to be behind you." And they both knew Simpleton's escape had resurrected the memories.

"It's hard for me to imagine that Cissy fell for his act," Lenora said as he drove toward her condo. "She had to have seen the news. Heard what he did to all those women."

And to her.

Micah's jaw twitched. "Some people are so lonely they only see what they want to see."

They drove the rest of the way in silence, Micah praying that the police spotted Simpleton's pickup and pulled him over so this nightmare could end for Lenora before it got worse.

A SIREN BLASTED THE air. Robert cursed as he looked up and saw a police car racing up behind him. Blue lights flashed and twirled, the lights nearly blinding him.

God dammit. He checked his speed. Under the limit. He hadn't run a stop sign, and there weren't any red lights in this lone stretch of highway.

Someone knew that he was driving this truck.

Fucking Cissy. He'd told her to throw away receipts, bills, anything that left a paper trail. But the stupid cunt obviously hadn't listened.

It was a good thing she was dead, or he'd kill her.

The police car roared closer, and he veered onto a side street and sped up, weaving around two other cars that were drag ass-ing along. He spotted another road up ahead to the right and skimmed the side of the VW as he passed, sending the driver toward the embankment. The VW spun out of control, causing the Jeep behind it to crash into its side, and he swung onto the other road just before the police car met up with the crash.

He whooped with joy when he saw the police car slow to see if the drivers were okay. Then he sped up and flew down the highway singing *Joy to the World*.

Images of Nan Purcell flashed in his head, and he clenched the steering wheel with a white-knuckled grip as his cock hard-ened. Nan had sat behind Lenora at his trial. Nan had been Le-nora's best friend since high school, and they'd roomed together in college.

But Nan had looked up at him, and he'd seen the doubts in her eyes. She didn't know whether to believe everything Lenora said.

She was drawn to him.

A smile tilted his lips as he remembered the file he'd obtained from another inmate who'd been paroled. It had burned in the diversionary fire at the prison, but he'd memorized every detail in it.

Nan was a financial planner. Traveled a lot. She lived alone.

He would have her tonight. That prim and proper, shy little lady was going to learn what it was like to be with a real man. What it was like to be loved.

What he'd done to Lenora.

But he'd wait to end her sorry life until Lenora was there to watch.

Listening to Lenora's pleas to save her friend would be his revenge. Then they would both have to die.

CHAPTER 5

ICAH SCANNED THE PARKING lot of Lenora's condo, half expecting to see the pickup Simpleton was driving but also knowing the man was smart and might park away from the complex and walk—rather *sneak*—inside.

Streetlights illuminated the lot, and he noticed two security cameras in opposite corners. She led him to her unit, a two-story with pansies in flowerboxes flanking the doorway.

Her hand shook as she unlocked the door, and he followed her inside, glad he kept a duffel bag of clothes and toiletries in his vehicle because he sure as hell didn't intend to leave her alone tonight.

A low light from a lamp on a side table enabled her to enter without totally being in the dark. After being held captive for so long, he wouldn't be surprised if she slept with a light on.

She turned to him in the foyer. Polished wood floors stretched across the large combination living room kitchen which was modern with a breakfast bar and white wooden stools. The room was painted a soft yellow, making it look airy and cheerful. "Thanks for driving me home, Micah."

"I'm not leaving you until Simpleton's back in prison," he said, determined she understand that he meant to keep his promise.

A slight seed of panic flared in her almond-shaped eyes. "That's not necessary, Micah. I have a security system."

"I know, but I'm still not leaving." He gestured toward the sofa. "Now I'd like to check out the rest of your condo before you turn in."

"Micah—"

"Please," he said in a gruff voice. "I made you a promise, and I intend to keep it."

She sighed, absentmindedly removing the clip holding her long blond hair at the nape of her neck. The gesture was so feminine and erotic that he had to draw a deep breath to keep from running his own hands through the silky looking strands that fell around her shoulders.

"All right." She led him to the stairs, and he followed her, noting the simple western landscapes on the wall.

"There are two bedrooms," she said, "although I use the second one as an office. There's a foldout couch in there."

A nice guest room, but he intended to stay downstairs in case Simpleton tried to break in. He glanced inside and saw nothing amiss. A desk with a laptop on it, bookcases with dozens of magazines and boxes labeled neatly, all related to her business. Samples of fabrics, photographs of flowers, wedding gowns, bridesmaids' dresses, lists of vendors and charts that she appeared to use to organize themed weddings.

She slipped into the master suite, a large space painted white with blue and green bedding on a brass bed. A club chair dominated the corner, and French doors opened to a terrace outside.

"This is my favorite part of the condo," Lenora said softly.

She opened the doors to a terrace with a wrought iron table, lounging chairs, and a hot tub. Stars glittered in the clear night sky, the moon beaming down on the porch offering a radiant glow as it shimmered over the woods behind the condo.

Lenora's face softened, her tension dissipating slightly. This was obviously the place she came to escape. A throw blanket lay on one of the chaises along with a pillow, and he realized that she probably slept out here sometimes.

To avoid the closed-in spaces and the nightmares?

He'd known soldiers who'd suffered PTSD from being confined during war. Some admitted they slept on the floor or outside because they needed air and space.

He hated Simpleton for taking Lenora's peace away from her. He wouldn't let the monster do it again.

Just letting Micah into her private sanctuary where she'd never brought a man, made Lenora feel exposed. Raw.

Needy.

For the first time in a long time, her heart fluttered with awareness, and she wondered what he thought of her home.

Of her.

"This is nice, Lenora. It looks like you've moved on."

Her gaze met his, questions simmering in his eyes.

"I know me being here is not what you want."

Except she did want him here. She only wished it was under different circumstances. "I appreciate you coming in person, Micah. You were good to me during the trial. That meant a lot."

"I was just doing my job," he said, although she'd secretly fantasized about a relationship. Not then. She hadn't been ready. But someday.

Then he'd left her with a simple goodbye, and she'd assumed she'd imagined any personal feelings between them. She had been a fragile wreck back then. She'd confused kindness with interest.

"You stood behind me during the worst time of my life," she said. "Not everyone did."

He clenched his jaw. "I know Simpleton's lawyer was rough. Out of line."

Her fiancé's betrayal was worse. "I guess he was just doing his job, too," she said. "Although I can't imagine why anyone would defend that horrible man."

Micah shrugged as if he had no answers. He certainly wouldn't have taken up for Simpleton. No, Micah was honorable and fought for what was right. Fought to protect others.

An image of Cissy Cornwell's dead body flashed in her mind, and a shudder rippled through her.

"Cold?" Micah asked.

She shook her head. "Just remembering tonight. Seeing that woman's body."

Micah hissed between his teeth. "Try not to think about it, Lenora. I'm not saying she deserved what he did to her, but she did help him escape."

"Because she thought he loved her." Her bitter laugh rent the air. "She was completely fooled by his act."

"Which means she had issues of her own. Anyone who watched the media circus surrounding Simpleton's arrest also saw the evidence against Simpleton. We had him dead to rights. He was—is—a cruel monster."

And he was on his way to kill her.

Lenora didn't say the words aloud. She didn't have to. They both knew it was true.

"Now try to get some rest. Maybe the police will track down that truck and in the morning we'll have him in custody."

She'd fantasize about that all night. But she'd lived the harsh reality of Simpleton, and she didn't believe fantasies came true.

"I'll be downstairs if you need me," Micah said, his dark eyes skating over her.

Lenora's pulse hammered. She did need him, wanted him to stay upstairs with her and hold her tonight.

But that meant she was weak. And using Micah as a crutch would only make it more difficult for her to cope when he left again.

And he would leave.

What man would want a life with a broken woman like her?

Micah fought images of Cissy's dead body in his mind because every time he saw her, Lenora's face appeared behind his eyes.

Lenora lying dead and bloody. Her eyes wide open in horror.

That damned bloody X carved on her chest.

He jogged down the steps, struggling to banish the images from his head. He was not going to let Lenora die.

He'd kill Simpleton first.

He checked his phone again, willing it to ring with the news that the police had apprehended Simpleton, but nothing happened. No messages in his inbox either.

Dammit.

He went to the kitchen, found a glass in the cabinet and filled it with water, then carried it to the window and drank as he glanced outside. The parking lot was dark and filled with cars, but he saw no movement.

The woods beyond loomed with possibilities, though. Even if there was security, the trees made it easier to gain access to the development.

The wind picked up, a storm brewing, sending leaves and twigs tumbling across the lot. A noise to the left caught his attention, and he studied the area, then spotted the silhouette of a man lighting a cigarette, leaning against a battered Jeep.

His body coiled with tension. Was it Simpleton? Had he found where Lenora lived? Was he stalking her now?

Antsy to know, he called upstairs to Lenora. "I'm going to

look around the parking lot. Stay inside with the door locked."

She appeared at the top of the steps, her face crinkled in worry. "Did you see someone?"

He shrugged. "Just routine. I want to check out the parking lot before we both turn in."

She nodded, but her hand tightened around the stair rail, and she slowly descended the steps. "I'll wait down here."

He stepped outside, waiting until she locked the door behind him, then he eased around the building to the corner where he'd seen the man. He had his back to him, coat collar pulled up, face obliterated in shadows.

Cigarette smoke curled into the sky as the man leaned his head back and blew smoke rings into the air. If it was Simpleton, he wasn't even trying to hide.

Cocky jerk.

Inching toward a van to disguise his actions until he could get a better look, Micah patted his gun, ready to draw. Out of the corner of his eye, he saw the man stiffen.

Micah walked slowly, so as not to startle him, but suddenly the man cursed, tossed the cigarette onto the ground, stubbed it out with the toe of his boot, then took off running along the edge of the parking lot.

Micah vaulted into action and ran after him. The man was tall, fast, wearing cowboy boots and jeans, but he couldn't distinguish his face. Moonlight streamed through the trees, enough for him to see a tattoo on the back of the man's neck.

His head was shaved, his body stout like Simpleton's.

The man dashed through a row of vehicles, then dove into a

black Range Rover. Micah sprinted in front of it, drew his gun and aimed it at the man's face.

"Get out or I'll shoot."

———————

ROBERT WATCHED THROUGH THE window of Nan Purcell's bedroom, his cock growing thicker as she shimmied into a little black dress. Was she going to a business dinner or was a lover waiting?

He wished he knew.

Not that it mattered.

He intended to change those plans for her.

Christ, she had great tits. He remembered them from the trial. Remembered that she'd worn a conservative white blouse, but that the buttons had strained across her big chest. The whole time he'd been on the stand, he'd stared at them, willing the buttons to pop and expose her cleavage.

He had imagined what her breasts looked like beneath that thin white blouse. The large dark areoles poking through a lacy white bra. White for purity.

Yet the bitch was not pure.

Those nipples begged for a man's mouth.

Would she scream when he touched her? Beg him to stop?

She straightened her skirt, long slender fingers running over her ass as she examined herself in the mirror.

He wanted to touch that ass himself. And he would.

She sank onto the stool in front of her vanity and began

combing through her dark hair. It was a deep reddish brown, shiny and long, wavy on the ends, curling around her neck. Her hand moved in nice even strokes.

Was she counting them?

His hands itched to thread the strands around his fingers. To wind them so tight she'd cry out in pain as he rammed himself inside her cunt.

Then she twisted her hair around one hand and slid a glittery comb in the bun to hold it away from her neck, exposing the creamy skin of her throat. He licked his lips, hungry to have her.

What would her skin taste like? Salty? Sweet like honey?

Excitement coursed through him.

Did she know he was out here watching? Maybe she did and she was putting on a show for him.

She turned sideways on the stool, slowly strapping on a pair of black-heeled sandals. Her toes were painted a deep crimson red.

Blood red.

Need shot through him, scorching hot. Heady.

Finally, she checked her make-up then picked up a tube of lipstick and painted her lips. The same color as her toenails.

Hot, delicious red again.

Smiling at herself, she spritzed perfume behind her ears, then a dot between her breasts.

Hmmm . . .

Satisfied with her looks, she grabbed her cell phone, jammed it inside a mini black purse, then sashayed from her bedroom to the living area.

He moved around the side of the house, slipping behind the bushes by her front door.

Stupid woman made it easy for him. She lived alone at the end of a street. He supposed she'd chosen the pretty little neighborhood thinking it was safe, that neighbors weren't far away.

They were far enough.

All tucked in their own houses with TVs blaring or heads buried in computers or their phones. No neighborhood watch here. In fact, his research indicated half of the homes had gone into foreclosure and were vacant.

She stepped onto the front stoop, then turned to lock the door, and he moved like lightning. She tried to scream as he grabbed her by the throat, but he used a paralyzing maneuver he'd learned in prison, and seconds later, she sagged in his arms.

He brushed her cheek with his lips as he carried her to the Honda he'd stolen after that fucking cop had nearly caught him in the truck. He opened the car door and settled Nan inside, smiling as she slumped down into the front seat.

"Soon we'll be back at my place." An Internet search at the library had allowed him to find an abandoned house not too far from Lenora that would work. A house just like the one he'd lived in as a child.

Back when the voices in his head had started.

He licked her neck. "Then the fun is going to begin, Nan. So much fun . . ."

CHAPTER 6

MICAH JERKED THE MAN by the collar of his shirt. "Who are you and what the hell are you doing stalking Lenora Lockhart?"

The man's eyes narrowed. They were set a little too close together, his nose was crooked, his teeth tobacco stained.

"I'm not stalking anybody, asshole. If you're here to shake me down for some money, I don't have any."

"It's Sgt. Hardin." Micah tapped the Silver Star on his shirt. "Texas Ranger."

"Oh, shit," the man muttered.

"Oh, shit, yeah," Micah growled. "Who do you owe money to?"

The man shrugged his beefy shoulders. "No one. You just looked like you wanted something. I figured it was money."

The man was nervous about something. "Why were you running? Someone hire you to find Lenora?"

"I told you I wasn't watching nobody," the man snarled. "I was just out for a smoke."

"Yeah, right. You live in that complex?"

"No."

"Girlfriend live there?"

The man lifted his chin. "No."

"Then what?" Micah dug into the man's pocket, yanked out his wallet, then flipped it open to look at his ID. Billy Willard, forty-five. "Either spill it or I'm locking you up. Probably gonna find a rap sheet, won't I?"

Willard cursed. "Look, I got into some trouble a while back, but I've been clean for months."

"What kind of trouble?"

"Just some petty stuff."

Micah tightened his hold. "How petty?"

"Jesus. A bag of weed, that's all."

Micah studied the man's eyes. They kept darting back toward the truck. "Is that why you were here? You buying dope?"

"Listen, man, I'm on parole. I can't go back to jail. They've got lunatics and murderers and rapists in there."

Micah relaxed slightly. "You weren't here looking for Lenora?"

An angry glint darkened Willard's eyes. "I don't know who this Lenora is, but no. I came here to make a deal. Period."

Micah released him. "Then get the hell out of here." He had to get back to Lenora himself.

Willard jumped in the Range Rover and roared from the parking lot.

Micah glanced around again, then strode back to Lenora's door and knocked. "It's Micah."

When the door swung open, relief spilled through him. She was safe for now.

He had to keep it that way.

———

LENORA LET MICAH IN, her heart hammering. She'd been worried sick that Simpleton had been outside and had hurt Micah. The crazy maniac had probably made friends in prison, ones she didn't want to meet. Hell, he was probably the leader of his own gang. Any one of them could be following her. "What happened?"

"False alarm," he said. "Guy ran because he was buying dope."

Relief whispered through her. "Thank God."

Micah nodded and squeezed her arm. "Go to bed and try to rest, Lenora."

His touch made her tingle all over. But that tingle frightened her in another way, so she hurried up the stairs. When she reached the landing, she paused and turned to look back at him. "Micah, you're welcome to sleep in my office."

"Thanks, but I'd rather stay down here so I can keep watch."

The reminder intensified her anxiety. She'd prefer he was upstairs with her, chasing away her nightmares.

But if he was downstairs, he would hear if someone tried to break in.

"THERE ARE SHEETS AND a pillow in the closet for the fold out. It's not very comfortable—"

"Trust me, I've slept on much worse."

His dark gaze pierced her, and he looked as if he wanted to say something, but he didn't. Instead, he walked back toward her living room.

She slipped into her room and closed the door, but as soon as she turned off the lights, the images flooded her. Dark images of the room where that monster had kept her, of his hands touching her, his mouth biting at her.

Suddenly she couldn't breathe. The room was stifling hot, the walls closing in, the sound of his footsteps shuffling as he came nearer echoing in her head.

She flipped the light back on, then moved out to the terrace. Desperate for air, she dragged in several deep breaths, then paced, forcing herself to look at the pale moon. The sky loomed above with glittering shapes that sparkled like diamonds.

Micah was downstairs. Only a few feet away.

Repeating the reminder in her head, she finally crawled onto the chaise, pulled the blanket over her, closed her eyes and let exhaustion claim her.

But in her sleep, the demons came.

Heavy breathing echoed in the silence. The rancid odor of her own sweat and the blood on her fingers where she'd clawed at Simpleton's arms when he'd tossed her in the cage. The cage that he'd kept her in before he took her to the house with the basement. A cage meant for an animal.

Bile rose in her throat as his odor permeated the air.

He smelled like sweat and dirty sex. His breath like stale beer. Cigarette smoke.

She gripped the bars of the cage, hating that he'd trapped her like a dog. Hating that she was helpless and weak and couldn't fight him off.

Hating that she'd begged like a baby for him to stop.

He fed on that weakness. On her tears and cries to release her. On the blood that he'd drawn from her when he'd cut her.

Another woman's shrill scream rent the air, the sound filled with terror.

Lenora buried her head in her hands and cried for the woman.

She knew what he was doing to her now.

That soon it would be her turn to die.

MICAH TENSED AT THE sound of a scream. He jumped up from the sofa, hand on his gun and raced up the steps. He had no idea how Simpleton could break in upstairs, but the man could have found a way. Maybe a rope or ladder . . .

His pulse pounded as he glanced inside Lenora's bedroom. She wasn't in bed. He ran to the bathroom, but it was empty. The terrace door was open.

He jogged to the door and quickly scanned the area, but he didn't see Simpleton anywhere.

Relief mingled with an ache in his chest when he saw Lenora twisting and turning in the midst of a nightmare on the chaise.

Except her nightmare was real. Memories that she'd tried to escape. Ones he'd resurrected when he'd informed her of Simpleton's escape.

Tamping down his emotions, he sank onto the chaise and pulled her in his arms. "Shh, Lenora, it's all right. It's over."

He stroked her hair, her back, her shoulders, gently whispering reassurances until finally she opened her eyes and looked up at him. The big luminous orbs were filled with tears, glazed with the pain of the past.

"You're safe now," he said softly. "Safe with me."

A flicker of something like trust danced in her eyes, replacing the haunted look, then she lay her head back against his chest and heaved a weary breath.

Compassion for her, along with other feelings he didn't want to acknowledge, filled him. He told himself that she was quiet now, calm, that he should leave.

Instead, he pulled her tighter up against him and held her until she fell asleep.

ROBERT HAD CARRIED NAN into his new house, a lovely old Victorian place with a basement that had been deserted years ago.

The cobwebs and dust motes gave the place a macabre feel, the dusty abandoned odor that permeated the rooms a reminder of the house he'd once lived in as a child.

Of the basement where he'd spent most of his time.

Ugly words rolled from his tongue as memories bombarded him—memories of his mother scrubbing his mouth with soap until his tongue was raw and bleeding. The ancient Victorian lamp in the corner looked exactly like the one she used to light up the room when she wanted him to see what was in her hands.

A belt. The thick rope used to hold back the heavy dark drapes. A cord she'd wind around his neck and penis.

Then the beating, and she'd close him in the dark.

Nan roused, a scream trying to escape the duct tape he'd stretched across her mouth, her eyes wide with fear.

She'd heard the stories Lenora had told in that fucking courtroom. She hadn't believed her best friend back then. Or maybe she had, but she'd been so delicate she hadn't been able to stand listening.

He would show her exactly what he'd done to Lenora. Make her a believer before he killed her.

She kicked at him as he carried her down the stairs, the cold, drafty walls rattling. The wind whistled through the eaves, dust motes swirling in front of his eyes as he plowed down the steps.

Nan was heavier than Lenora, a fighter, too.

That would make it more fun.

But he wanted Lenora here for the party to watch him take his pleasure from her friend.

Nan squirmed and wiggled, kicking and trying to elbow him, but he kicked open the door to one of the rooms and tossed her inside. Her body clunked as it hit the concrete floor, a grunt of pain escaping her.

Darkness bathed the room, the light snuffed out by a lack of windows, the musty scent of age, rotting wood and dead animal so strong that he paused to inhale it.

Home sweet home. Just like when he was young.

He was tempted to stay here and keep Nan company tonight, but he had other plans. He had to find his second victim quickly.

Then it would be time for Lenora to join them.

Hand on his cock, rubbing, stroking, he limped toward Nan, his shoes scraping the concrete.

She shook her head wildly, her eyes huge with horror and denial. He removed the burner phone from his pocket, then punched in Lenora's phone number. Adrenaline sped through his veins as he waited on her to answer.

One ring. Two. Three.

"Come on, my pet," he whispered. "Talk to me. I've been waiting..."

***

LENORA JERKED AWAKE, EMBARRASSMENT heating her cheeks as she woke in Micah's arms. His dark eyes met hers, a softness about them that made desire bubble in her belly.

She hadn't been close to anyone, especially a man, in years.

She'd thought she would hate it, that she'd run from his touch.

But somehow, having Micah beside her, so close, so strong and tough yet so gentle, not demanding but protecting, made her crave more.

He made her want to be whole again. To be able to find love and a future that she'd given up on five years ago.

"Lenora—"

The sound of her phone ringing cut into the moment, and she shoved hair from her face. It was barely dawn. Who would be calling?

"My phone—"

He hurried into her room and retrieved it from the nightstand.

"It's an unknown number," he said with a frown.

"Maybe it's him."

"I'll answer—"

"No, he wants to talk to me." She grabbed the phone, then pressed the answer button. "Hello."

A tense silence echoed over the line, then a breath.

"Who is this?"

"Lenora," a woman's voice cracked.

Fear crawled through Lenora. "Nan?"

"Help me," Nan cried. "He's got me . . ."

A scream followed, then Robert Simpleton's sinister laugh exploded over the line.

CHAPTER 7

MICAH CAUGHT LENORA AS she doubled over with a groan. "Oh, god, oh, god, oh, god . . ."

"What is it, Lenora? Was that him?"

Tears glittered in her tormented eyes as she looked up at him. "Yes. No . . . Nan . . . it was Nan."

"Nan?"

"My friend . . . he has her."

Fury shot through Micah, and he stroked a strand of hair from her damp cheek. "What did she say?"

Lenora's nails dug into his arms through his shirtsleeves. "That he had her . . . then she screamed."

Lenora collapsed in his arms, and he closed his eyes, battling his rage as she purged her emotions. Her body trembled with the force, his own shaking with the effort to control himself when he wanted to punch a wall.

And to kill Simpleton.

He wished to hell that he'd killed the son of a bitch instead of turning him into the police for prosecution.

He rocked Lenora in his arms, knowing she needed time to absorb the shock. But he needed to get to work. To find the bastard.

"Nan…he'll hurt her," Lenora cried. "I know what he'll do…"

"Shh," he murmured. "We're going to find him."

She shuddered against him, her eyes red-rimmed and swollen. "But how? And how much will she have to suffer first?" She sucked in a breath, sniffling as she worked to regain control. "He's doing this to her because of me."

Micah forced her to look at him. "Listen to me, Lenora, this is not your fault."

"It is," she said raggedly. "He's punishing me for testifying against him. He's coming for me, but he's going to hurt people I care about first just to torture me."

Unfortunately, he couldn't argue. She knew Simpleton better than anyone.

Which meant she might be able to help.

It would be painful, but she might actually be able to offer insight into the way his thought processes worked.

"Stop. I know you're worried about her and that Simpleton is a monster, but you need to pull it together, Lenora, so we can find her."

Her lower lip quivered, then she took another breath and wiped at her eyes with the back of her hand. "You're right. What should we do?"

"I'm going to call the office and see if the tech department can trace where that call came from." It was probably a dead end. Most criminals knew to use burner cells and Simpleton was smart. But he had to try.

"I want you to think. Did you hear anything else on the line?"

Her eyes drew together in thought. "No . . . just Nan. She was crying. Scared." Her voice cracked. "She knows what he did to me, what's going to happen."

"Shh," he said again, then massaged her shoulder. "Think about it, Lenora. Maybe you heard a siren in the background. A car horn? A train?"

She rubbed her temple and closed her eyes as if struggling to recall the details. When she opened them, she looked defeated. "I did hear a muffled sound . . . maybe a plane in the distance."

"So he might have taken her somewhere near an airport."

"I barely heard it," she said. "I don't think it was near a major airport."

"There are smaller ones in the country, private airfields." He squeezed her arm. "That's good, Lenora. That might help."

"Did Nan have any family we should notify?"

"No," Lenora said, her voice strained. "She lost her parents in a car accident two years ago."

He snatched up his phone and pressed the number for the tech department at the Ranger's office. "It's Hardin. Did you find anything on Cissy Cornwall's phone records?"

"Nothing helpful. Just calls to the prison."

"We just heard from Simpleton. I need you to trace a call

for me." He gave the tech Lenora's number and the time of the call then waited.

Lenora rose from the chaise, walked to the edge of the terrace and looked out over the woods. Her tormented expression bothered him. She was still blaming herself. Reliving what Simpleton had done to her because she thought her friend was being abused in the same way now.

He cursed beneath his breath, hating the helpless feeling engulfing him. The sicko never should have seen the light of day again.

Seconds later, the tech came back on the line. "Sorry. The caller used a burner cell."

Dammit. "Keep a trace on Lenora's phone in case he calls back. Maybe if we record it, we'll hear something in the background." Micah's mind raced. "Also, search for small private airfields outside Austin. Send the coordinates to me and send a tech team to Nan Purcell's house."

"I'll get right on it."

Micah hung up, then walked over to Lenora. "Come on, let's shower and get coffee. We'll meet the crime team at Nan's place in case Simpleton left a clue there for us."

Her eyes widened. "You think he'd do that intentionally?"

"He wants you," Micah said, a muscle ticking in his jaw. "He's either going to ambush us or leave you breadcrumbs so you'll come to him."

LENORA HADN'T CONSIDERED THAT Simpleton would try to lead her to him. But she hoped he did. Then she and Micah could make him pay for kidnapping her friend.

Nan . . . God help her. Would she survive?

She forced her mind away from the dark path and darted into the bedroom, then into the bath to shower. But the disturbing thoughts returned as the hot water pummeled her.

Memories of Simpleton's hands on her, his rough nails clawing at her as he pushed her legs apart and shoved himself inside her. His rancid breath on her skin when he'd ordered her to lie on her stomach or drop to her knees . . .

The old familiar dirty feeling haunted her. Her obsession with scrubbing herself took a life if its own, and she found herself vigorously washing and scrubbing her chest, determined to make that hideous X disappear forever.

But as the water cooled, and she finally turned off the faucet and dried her body, the X remained. The plastic surgeon her mother had hired had smoothed over the torn jagged skin, had insisted it was invisible now.

But she could see it. It would always be with her. Always be a reminder that she was battered and damaged. That she would never be whole again.

Especially not when he was out there, torturing her friend, and waiting to finish her.

———————

MICAH PHONED LT. ROPER and relayed the news about Nan Purcell as he and Lenora drove toward the woman's home. "We need to get a photo of her out to the press and across the police databases ASAP."

"I'll pull her driver's license picture," Lt. Roper said. "How's Lenora taking it?"

"How do you think?" Micah said. "The monster abducted her friend to punish her."

"We'll get him," Lt. Roper said.

But when? And would they locate him before he tortured Nan?

"Lenora thought she heard a small plane in the background when Nan called," Micah said. "I asked tech to send me a list and coordinates of any small airfields outside Austin."

"We'll start looking for cabins or houses that are abandoned or in isolated areas, too. We know how Simpleton thinks. He'll take the victims some place off the grid."

So no one could hear the women scream.

"Send me whatever you get. We're on our way to Nan's now. Maybe a neighbor saw something."

"Keep me posted," his boss said.

Micah pocketed his phone, and Lenora twisted her hands in her lap. "I haven't seen or talked to Nan in years," she said in a pained voice. "We lost touch after the trial."

When Lenora had needed her most. Lenora must have felt abandoned.

"Simpleton may not know that," he said. "He probably saw her at the trial and knew you two were close."

"Nan couldn't handle hearing details about what happened to me," Lenora said. "Even if he doesn't kill her, I don't know if she'll survive emotionally."

Micah squeezed her hand. "Maybe we'll find her before he hurts her."

Lenora's face grew strained as if she wanted to latch onto the hope he offered, but she couldn't. She wasn't a naïve young girl. Simpleton had robbed any innocence from her and shown her the darkest side of mankind.

And Simpleton had already traumatized Nan by kidnapping her.

Micah turned down the drive to Nan's place, noting the neatly kept lawns and expensive cars in the drive.

"Have you been to Nan's house?" Micah asked.

Lenora shook her head. "She used to live in an apartment. It looks like she's done well for herself."

"What does she do for a living?"

"She's a financial planner, always planning for the future." Her voice cracked. "A future she might not have now because of me."

"Not because of you," Micah said firmly. "Because a sick, twisted murderer escaped from prison."

"I appreciate that you're trying to make me feel better, Micah, but we both know the truth."

He reached the end of the street and turned into the drive. A black BMW sat in front, then his gaze fell to the purse lying on the ground and a scarf that must have belonged to Nan.

This was where Simpleton had abducted her.

The crime unit would arrive any minute. He wanted every bit of evidence possible to make sure the man paid for his crimes.

CHAPTER 8

Lenora tamped down her emotions as she slid from the car. Nan's purse and scarf were on the ground. One of her black heels was lying in the grass as if it had been kicked aside.

Probably when she'd tried to fight Simpleton.

God.

"Don't touch anything, Lenora. A crime unit is on the way," Micah said.

"We know who did it."

"But we need forensics to back up the case."

She whirled on Micah. "You mean in case she's dead and he doesn't confess?"

Tension stretched between them for a full second.

"Trust me, Lenora. This time he'll get death row."

She regretted taking her frustration out on him. Micah

was trying to help, doing his best to take care of her and find Simpleton.

"I'm sorry," she said. "I'm just on edge."

"No apology needed." Micah offered her a smile. "I know this is difficult."

"All the more reason to do everything we can to find Nan." She glanced inside the car, but nothing looked amiss. He must have been watching Nan, jumped her when she came out to her car.

The front door stood ajar, and she slowly walked toward it, but Micah caught her arm. "Let me search the house first."

Fear shot through her, and she glanced around the driveway for blood or a body but didn't see any. "You think Nan might be inside? Or that he might be?"

Micah's shoulders lifted in a slight shrug. "I don't know, but we can't take any chances."

Her pulse pounded as he pulled his weapon and inched inside the house. She wished she'd brought her own gun.

The house was a small one-story with an open layout, a large den connecting to the kitchen. Nice wood flooring, expensive cream-colored couches, an office to the right visible from the living area.

"Everything looks in order in here," Micah said.

Every muscle in Lenora's body tensed as she followed him down the hallway past the office. What if Nan's body was here?

What if he'd raped and tortured her in her own home knowing she and Micah would search the house?

Plush white carpet covered the floor of the master bedroom,

a queen bed dominated the room, and the closet was open, revealing an array of suits and designer outfits.

Thankfully Nan wasn't inside the room.

The sound of water trickling echoed from the bathroom and Lenora's breath caught. God, no . . .

Simpleton had enjoyed shoving his victims below the icy water in the bath, forcing them under for so long they would be chilled inside, lose the will to live and beg to die. Then he would do it again.

But in the end, he'd revive them, use his precious knife to stab them in the heart and carve an X in their chest

An image of Nan lying on the bathroom floor covered in blood flashed in her mind, and Lenora gripped the wall, unable to look as Micah entered the room.

MICAH EXHALED IN RELIEF at the sight of the empty bathroom. The water in the tub was dripping, the tub full and starting to overflow, so he turned off the water.

"He used to dunk us in an ice bath and hold us down until we choked and lost our breath," Lenora said behind him.

He scrubbed a hand over his face, blotting out the image.

Had Simpleton left the water running to remind Lenora of his sick twisted ways?

Demented asshole.

Lenora was trembling, so he clasped her hand and led her back through the house. She paused at the bookshelf and stared at the framed photographs arranged on the shelf. Several of Nan and an older man he assumed was her father, then a picture of Lenora and Nan.

The two of them stood side by side in front of the college in their caps and gowns, their arms linked as they showed off their diplomas.

"I can't believe she still has that picture."

Micah cleared his throat. "Maybe she just didn't know how to help you after the trial," Micah said. "When some people suffer tragedies or undergo traumatic experiences, it changes them. The people around them often don't know what to do or say."

"I know I changed, I was difficult to be around," Lenora said softly. "I don't blame her for pulling away."

He rubbed her arms to warm her. "That's not what I meant. She was your friend. She let you down when you needed her most. That's hard to forgive."

Pain wrenched her face, but outside, the sound of an engine cut through the air, and Micah released her. "That's probably the crime van."

He hurried outside to meet them and explained their suspicions. "Look for hair fibers, fingerprints, anything we can use to prove that Simpleton was here."

The team went to work, and he ushered Lenora back to the car. "I want to look over the files and transcripts from the trial," Micah said. "Simpleton was interviewed by a court-appointed shrink. Talking to her might give us some insight where he might take Nan."

"We know it'll be an isolated area, an abandoned house or building, someplace with a basement that's dark," Lenora said, her voice regaining strength.

"Yes, but there might be some other detail that we missed that might help narrow it down. Maybe a special childhood place, an area that meant something to him."

"Call her and let's go see her," Lenora said.

The silence was deafening as he sped away. A few miles down the road, he spotted a coffee shop and pulled in. "I have those files in my trunk. I can look at them and find the number of that psychiatrist while we have coffee."

Lenora's cell phone dinged, and she snatched it from her purse. When she glanced at the caller ID screen, her face crumpled.

"What?"

She handed him the phone and he read the text.

> *Dearest Lenora,*
> *One for the party. One to go.*
> *Soon it's time you joined the show.*
> *Love and kisses,*
> *Robert*

Micah cursed and pulled Lenora up against him, then wrapped his arm around her

shoulders as he escorted her inside. They ordered coffee and muffins, and he laid his briefcase on the table.

"Who is he going after next?" Lenora said in a haunted voice.

"You tell me. Who else are you close to?"

"No one except Jenny," she said. "And I already warned her."

"Has she left town yet?"

"I think she was stopping by today to turn things over to Wilma before she left." Panic flared in her eyes. "I'd better check in."

She punched her friend's number while he opened the file and scanned it.

Lenora had been Simpleton's only survivor so her testimony had been key to the prosecution. Other evidence was muddy due to a mix up at a lab and Simpleton's ability to cover his ass. Damn crime shows. Between them and the Internet, perps could virtually find a textbook lesson on how to get away with murder.

"What? Listen, Jenny, I don't like that you're there alone. I'll come right over."

Micah frowned. He was surprised Troy left her alone for a minute, but Jenny seemed as stubborn as Lenora and probably insisted.

"That man already kidnapped one of my friends from college. I don't know who he's coming after next, but I'm worried about you." A pause. "Okay, keep the door locked. And call me as soon as Troy comes back."

Lenora tapped her fingernails on her coffee cup when she hung up.

"She's there alone?"

"Yes," Lenora said. "Troy went to get them some food and should be back any minute."

"Take a deep breath, and call back in a few minutes. If he's not back, we'll go over there."

"I'd feel better if we went now," Lenora said.

He'd do anything for her. "All right." He closed the file just as her phone jangled again.

"Jenny?" Another pause. "Okay, great. Now close up the shop and go some place safe with Troy."

She looked relieved when she hung up. "Do you see anything in the file?"

"Here's the shrink's name and contact information," Micah called the number and spoke to her secretary. "I need to see Dr. Rowan." He identified himself and explained the situation, and she told him to come as soon as possible.

Lenora stood. "Let's go."

Fifteen minutes later, they were seated in the doctor's office. Dr. Rowan was tall and slim with a short, dark bob of hair and square glasses. Thankfully she worked with the police and courts, so privilege wasn't a problem. With a woman's life hanging in the balance, she had to talk to them anyway. "I heard about Simpleton's escape," she said.

"We need insight to find him. What can you tell us?"

"Robert Simpleton was severely abused as a child. His mother was schizophrenic and treated him horribly. She punished him with beatings, using anything she could find from a broomstick or belt to tree limbs to whip him. She used to make him cut his own switch for her to use."

The woman paused, her short fingernails drumming over the man's file. "She filled a bathtub of cold water and dunked him over and over as another punishment. He lost consciousness more than once, but managed to survive." Her brows drew together. "Of course he was scarred permanently."

"She raped him?"

Dr. Rowan nodded. "Repeatedly. Again she used various objects. She also allowed men to come in and use him. She . . . was amused by it."

Lenora massaged her temple as if the doctor's comments were disturbing her. As if she had sympathy for Simpleton.

He didn't feel sorry for the asshole. Sure, Simpleton had a tough childhood and shouldn't have been abused, but that didn't justify his abuse against innocent women.

"In my opinion, the women he tortured personify his mother," Dr. Rowan continued. "He's finally getting his revenge against her for what she did to him."

"We're trying to figure out where he's holding Nan Purcell," Micah said. "Is there anything in his background that might help us? Maybe a specific place his mother used to take him? Some place meaningful?"

Lips pursed in thought, the doctor opened the file and skimmed her finger along a section. Seconds later, she lifted out a childlike drawing of an old Victorian house that looked haunted.

"This is a sketch of the house he grew up in, where his trauma first occurred," she said. "If Mr. Simpleton believes this is his last chance to punish his mother, he might want to recreate the same setting where he was abused himself for his victims."

ROBERT HAD BEEN WATCHING Jenny, the girl who worked with Lenora, but some big oaf of a guy was dogging her like she was in heat. He'd have to wait till the creep left her or . . . find some-one else who fit his needs.

He turned on the faucet in the tub in the basement and watched the water begin to trickle. It hadn't been used in ages and was rusty and spewed brown water, just like the one in his childhood home.

His lungs squeezed for air, the familiar panic and adrenaline mingling as images of the baptisms formed in his mind. That was what his mama called them.

Punishments. Lessons. Cleansings of the soul.

The drip, drip, drip of the water made him smile. The tub was nearly full now. The water icy cold just as it was when his mama baptized him.

Now it was Nan's turn to be punished. To be saved.

The darkness greeted him like a safe haven as he headed to the room to get her.

Somewhere in the darkness, a mouse skittered. Old pipes rattled. The wind beat at the shutters.

He removed the key from his waist and unlocked the door to Nan's room. She lay deathly still in the corner, her hands and feet still bound, her hair tangled around her.

Feet moving on autopilot, he shuffled to her and gripped her by the hair. She jerked her eyes open and tried to scream, but the duct tape drowned the sound.

Smiling, he ripped the tape off, knowing no one would hear her cries. They were too isolated.

Her eyes went buggy with terror, and she tried to fight him again, sending his pulse into an uproar. He dragged her up the stairs, then started to undress her.

She kicked and pushed at him with her body, and he slapped her, ripped off that little black dress, and stripped her down to her lace panties.

Those would come off later.

For now, he shoved her into the water. Her scream of shock at the icy temperature echoed in the air like music. Grinning, he pushed her under, counting the seconds as she flailed and struggled.

CHAPTER 9

ICAH PHONED THE TECH team as he and Lenora settled back inside his SUV. "I'm still waiting for you to send me that list of airfields."

"It's on its way. But there are several."

"Maybe we can narrow it down. Look for older Victorian houses that might be abandoned or for sale or rent within close proximity of those airports." He snapped his fingers. "Better yet, do we have the address of Simpleton's childhood house?"

A second passed, then the tech gave him an address.

Micah cleared his throat. "I'll check that out while you look for others."

"It'll take a little while."

"Make it quicker. Simpleton already abducted one woman. He sent Lenora a text saying one more and then he's coming after her. He's probably choosing the second victim as we speak."

"I'll send you what I find."

"Thanks." Micah hung up and called his friend Mitchell Manning. "I'm working the Simpleton case, Mitch. He kidnapped a friend of Lenora's, and we're looking for a place where he's holding her. The shrink who evaluated Simpleton suggested he might return to a house similar to the one he grew up in. Tech is searching now and should be sending me a list to check soon. But first I'm going to check out his childhood home."

"Look, man, you know I'm not working now."

"I know, Mitch, but maybe getting back to work would help." Mitch had lost his wife and kid to the job nine months before. Micah was worried about him. Grieving was normal, but Mitch had been the most driven ranger he'd ever known.

He'd lost that drive when he'd buried his wife and child.

"If he's not at that house, I'm going to need a chopper."

"Hardin—"

"This woman's life depends on it, Mitch."

Tension stretched between them. "All right. Call me if you need the chopper and I'll meet you at the ranch."

"Where are you are now?"

"My place. Getting ready to put the damn thing on the market."

Micah's gut tightened. Mitch loved that ranch. But it probably held painful memories for him.

Micah thanked him, disconnected and headed out of town. It was a long shot that Simpleton would actually carry Nan to his home, but it fit his profile.

Right now Micah had no other place to look.

LENORA STUDIED THE SCENERY, the long stretch of road echoing with the sound of wild animals and her own fear. Cacti, trees and deserted property looked stark with dry parched weeds and grass.

Every second that passed was tormented by images of the pain Nan might be enduring.

Occasionally they passed a farm or ranch, although many were no longer working ranches or farms. "Are we close?" she asked as a sign for a place called Four Horses swayed in the breeze.

"A few more miles." Micah glanced at her with raised brows. "Are you okay?"

She shook her head. "How can I be, knowing that Nan is suffering?"

He squeezed her hand, and for once, Lenora allowed herself to cling to it. As a child, her mother had been totally dependent on Lenora's father, and she'd fallen apart when he'd died.

Lenora had vowed never to be that needy.

Still, she couldn't let go of Micah's hand.

The SUV bounced over potholes, slinging rocks and dust. Suddenly, he turned down a dirt drive, weaving around a fallen tree and limbs that had been ripped from the trunks and tossed across the road. A big dip in the road made him swerve again.

"Are you sure this is right?" Lenora asked.

He checked his GPS. "Yeah. Remember, this is where Simpleton grew up. No one has lived here in years."

A shiver rippled up her spine. It would make a perfect place to hide.

"There are recent tire marks, too," Micah said, pointing to various ridges in the dry ground.

"So he might have brought Nan out here." Lenora's pulse picked up a notch. She silently prayed he was here, that they could end this now and save Nan.

In the distance, an old Victorian house popped into view, dark clouds painting the turrets and sharp angles in eerie shadows. Lenora scanned the yard and drive for a vehicle, hoping to find the truck Robert had been driving. Instead, a rusty, broken-down Chevy sat on cinder blocks beside the house.

"I don't see his truck," she said, her hope deflating.

"He could have stashed it around back or left Nan here and be out hunting again."

Her anxiety rose as he slowed and came to a stop beneath a cluster of trees. The afternoon sun was fading, gray skies obliterating the sun and adding a dismal cast to the sky.

A bird cawed, a coyote howled, and vultures fluttered and soared above a patch of land in the distance.

Micah cut the engine, and she reached for the door, but he pressed a hand over hers. "Wait here and let me check out the house, Lenora."

"No, I'm coming with you. If Nan is in there alone, she'll need me."

Micah's gaze met hers and his jaw tightened. "Okay, but stay behind me. And if he's in there and starts shooting, run like hell to the car and call for help."

She agreed, hoping it didn't come to that.

———————

MICAH HELD HIS GUN at the ready as he approached the weathered old house. Peeling paint, rotting shingles, and broken windowpanes confirmed that the place was deserted and had been for a long time.

Birds had nested on the front porch, and he glanced through one of the front windows and saw that the lights were off. Sheets had been draped over furniture, and dust and cobwebs clung to everything in sight. A hint of mold crept up the wall on the right side of the living room.

He turned the front door knob, and it screeched open. A musty odor engulfed him, the smell of a house that hadn't been inhabited in years. His gaze swept to the dining room to the side and a parlor. Both vacant although signs of rodents were evident in droppings and gnawed furniture legs.

Lenora's breath puffed out as she followed him to the kitchen. A broken down table sat on three legs, and layers of dirt and grime coated the ancient appliances. A spider had spun an elaborate web along the light fixture above the table.

But no one was inside, and it didn't look as if anyone had been recently.

He gestured toward the hallway, and they slowly climbed the stairs, the wood bending and squeaking beneath their feet. A noise echoed from above, and his heart jumped. Was someone upstairs?

Lenora touched his arm, and he lifted his finger to his mouth to remind her to keep quiet. He crept down the hall, looked inside the first room and noted an empty iron bed that had been stripped of any bedding. A worn dresser sat on the far wall. He glanced in the closet but it was empty.

No clothing inside as if the family had moved abruptly but forgotten to come back for their furniture. He quickly checked the bathroom and found it dirty but empty as well.

The noise sounded again as if something was banging against a window. He motioned for her to follow, and they inched their way to the next room. This room was even more drab than the others and appeared to be a child's room.

A small twin bed was covered in a faded navy bedspread that hung askew. Toy cars had been dumped on the floor along with yellowed, tattered books. A stain marred the dingy beige carpet, a stain that looked like blood.

"This was his room," Lenora whispered.

Micah took note of the belt hanging on the wall, a wide leather belt that had probably been used to punish Simpleton as a child. Micah eased toward the bathroom and found the source of the noise.

A bird was trapped inside, flying back and forth, slamming into the wall and the window as it tried to escape. Had Robert Simpleton felt like that bird in this house?

Micah covered his head with one hand, eased over to the window and shoved it open, giving the bird its freedom.

Lenora pointed to the tub. A bloodstain marred the cracked porcelain. "That must have been where she punished him."

"She was demented," Micah said. "But that doesn't excuse what he did to you or give him the right to murder and rape innocent women."

"He didn't see us as innocent," Lenora said. "When he looked at us, he saw her face."

"Then he should have checked himself into a mental hospital." He gripped her arm. "Come on, let's see if there's a basement."

They hurried down the stairs and found a doorway in the hall that led to more stairs. It was so dark that Micah pulled a penlight from his pocket to light the way.

Dust motes danced in front of him, the scent of something rancid filling the air.

"God . . . what is that?" Lenora whispered.

"A dead rat probably." The stairs squeaked, and one collapsed, making him grip the rail. "Careful." He took Lenora's hand and helped her over it, then shined the penlight across the small cement space. The ceiling was low, cinder blocks comprising the walls. An antique trunk sat to the left, a metal cage in the corner.

The defense attorney apparently hadn't had photos of this place or he would have used them in Simpleton's defense.

Lenora gasped, her hand clutching at his arm. "I think I'm going to be sick."

The cage looked like a dog cage but reminded him of the one Lenora had described. Apparently, Simpleton had held Lenora in a cage when he'd first abducted her. No wonder she felt ill.

But his eyes were glued to the trunk. What if Simpleton had stuffed Nan's body in that trunk?

ROBERT LEFT NAN TO rest, smiling to himself at the way she'd begged for her life. He'd told her that he'd release her once he had Lenora. Of course, that was a lie.

She would die just as Lenora would.

But first things first.

He walked through Lenora's mother's house, running a finger along the dust-free furniture. Everything looked as if it had been spit-polished. Furniture was new, magazines stacked neatly on the shiny coffee table. Kitchen immaculate, refrigerator full of fresh vegetables, fruit and expensive cuts of meat. The rooms even smelled like spring flowers.

Nothing like the home where he'd grown up. Dirty floors and tables, grimy kitchen, day-old bread and outdated canned food his mother had picked up at a salvage store.

A tree branch scraped the window outside, and he froze, remembering the times his mother had shoved him outdoors, tied him to a tree and left him out in the storm. Discipline meant punishment.

Punishment meant that she loved him.

Just like he loved Lenora and the other women he'd taken. They had to be punished just as he had.

That was the only way they would get into heaven.

He paused and studied a photograph of Lenora and her

mother, the two of them sitting side by side for a Christmas shot when Lenora was a teenager. Something about the picture made him think that the two weren't close. Lenora's tight smile?

The distance between them, as if they didn't want to physically touch.

Her mother had seemed cold and distant at the trial, too. She'd avoided reporters. Sat gripping a handkerchief to her face, crying quietly.

He had watched her carefully. Pain had wrenched Lenora's face at her mother's reaction.

He spotted a family album, picked it up and thumbed through it. Photos of Lenora as a baby and toddler, a big burly man holding her, smiling, the two of them laughing. In one picture, the mother hung all over the man while Lenora sat a body length away. Another one showed the three of them, once again the father holding Lenora, the mother pulling the man toward her. Had she been jealous of her husband's attention toward their daughter?

He paused at a shot of Lenora standing beside a grave. Her mother was there, head bent, face in shadows. The tombstone marker belonged to Lenora's father.

After that, there were very few pictures of Lenora. Had her mother abandoned her daughter in her grief?

Yes, she was not the mother his had been. Maybe they hadn't had the perfect house, the nicest furniture, and meals, but in her own way, she'd loved him.

She'd told him that over and over every time she'd beaten him or given him an ice bath.

A car engine sounded outside, and he ducked into the woman's bedroom. The sound of the front door unlocking echoed from the living room, then voices. Two women's.

He peeked through the crack in the doorway and watched them.

"I'm fine now," Lenora's mother said. "Go on home tonight, Gladys."

"But what about that madman?"

"Lenora was just being paranoid. He's not coming after me," Mrs. Lockhart said. "All the women he kidnapped were young, in their twenties."

"That's true," the other woman said. "But still, I hate to leave you alone."

"Nonsense," Mrs. Lockhart said as she strode to the bar and poured herself a glass of wine. "I'm exhausted. I'll set the alarm and go to bed. I'll call you in the morning."

"If you're sure." Gladys hugged Mrs. Lockhart then let herself out.

Robert smiled as Lenora's mother sipped her wine and headed toward the bedroom. He slipped inside the closet and pulled the door shut. He'd wait until she was settled in bed.

Then he'd introduce himself to her firsthand.

Wouldn't she be surprised that her age didn't matter?

In fact, she was about the age of his own mother. When he closed his eyes, their faces blended.

"Yes, Mama," he whispered. "I'll take care of her."

Her laughter rang in his ears, followed by the sound of a hard slap as she hit him with the paddle. He was supposed to take it over and over.

His cock swelled at the thought. She liked to hear him cry and beg and scream.

But he was never supposed to come.

He did it anyway. Felt his release building with each slap on his ass. He couldn't help it. He spewed his cum everywhere.

Of course, she beat him for that, too.

So many times, he'd wanted to turn her over and spray his fluids all over her.

This time he would. He'd enjoy his release while Lenora watched.

Then it would be her turn to pleasure him.

CHAPTER 10

Lenora's lungs churned for air as Micah walked toward the antique trunk. Dank air swirled around her, adding to the threatening nausea.

What if Nan was in that trunk?

Dear God, no . . .

Micah knelt to examine the lock on the trunk, then yanked at it. Metal clanged against metal, but it didn't budge.

"I need a crowbar or something to break this lock," Micah said.

Lenora jerked from her stupor and searched the right side of the basement while he looked around the left. Tension vibrated between them, the clock ticking. If Nan was inside that trunk, she could be hurt. Barely breathing.

Dead.

"Here, how about this ax?" She shuddered at the sight of something dark on the edges that looked like blood.

"That'll work." He held it above the lock and swung it down, hacking at it until the lock popped open. Then he tossed the lock to the floor and lifted the lid of the trunk. Images of Nan hurt, bloody from that ax, pummeled Lenora, and she couldn't look.

"Micah?"

His breath hissed out. "She's not inside."

Relieved, Lenora turned around to see for herself. The trunk was filled with an array of items. An old football that had a hole in it. A pair of mud-crusted sneakers.

Boy's clothing that looked soiled and smelled rotten. A blood-soaked rag. Cloth bandages that reeked.

"Mementos of Simpleton that his mother kept?" Micah muttered.

"If he hadn't turned out to be so cruel, I'd feel sorry for him," Lenora said in a low voice.

"How did she die?" Micah asked.

Lenora shrugged. "He never said. He just said he wished he'd killed her."

"What about his father?"

"He said he left them when he was little."

"The old man probably figured out he was married to a freak."

Lenora shuddered. The smell seemed to have grown stronger. "Let's get out of here."

Micah lifted his head and scanned the room once again.

"Wait. There's a wardrobe behind that mattress."

Lenora hadn't noticed it, but once again terror seized her at the possibility of her friend's body being inside.

Micah carried the ax over to the wardrobe and hacked away the lock at the top. Dark shadows shrouded the tall piece of furniture as the doors screeched open. Suddenly the rancid odor swirled thicker, making Lenora gag.

"Oh, my god, what is that?"

"I think we just found Simpleton's father."

MICAH CURSED THEN CLOSED the wardrobe door, hoping to shield Lenora. But when he glanced back at her pale face, he realized she'd seen the skeleton.

He wondered why the house hadn't been searched during the trial but assumed no one had discovered it.

"What makes you think that's the father?" Lenora asked.

"Just a hunch," Micah said. "Father went missing. Maybe he didn't run off. Maybe the crazy wife killed him, then abused her son."

Lenora inched closer to the stairs, whispers of ghosts echoing in the silence.

"I need to call a crime team." He took her arm and coaxed her back up the stairs, and outside onto the front porch.

She walked over to the SUV and leaned against it, obviously needing air. He made the call and explained the situation. "You'll need to transport the bones back for identification. I want COD and TOD when you get it." Not that they could arrest Simpleton's mother since she was dead.

But what if Robert Simpleton had actually killed his father and hid his body in that wardrobe? Maybe the mother's abuse against her son stemmed with rage over what the son had done?

He decided to look around the property while he waited on the crime team, so he circled the house. In the back, he found a storage shed. He looked inside and found an old rusted lawnmower, a metal tub filled with compost, and various pesticides and poisons.

Had Simpleton been poisoned as part of his abuse?

The hiss of a snake made him freeze, and he slowly backed out of the shed, grateful when the crime van rolled down the hill.

He met the team as they exited the van. Lenora remained by the SUV, her arms folded, as he escorted the team inside to show them what he'd found.

He explained his theory. "I need the body identified, TOD and COD, as soon as possible. Also, see if you find any recent prints or blood, and send me the results."

He thanked them and returned to Lenora. "Come on, let's go."

Protectively, he placed his hand to her waist, then opened the car door and Lenora sank inside, her expression tormented.

Nan had been with Simpleton for hours now. No telling what he was doing to her.

Lenora looked exhausted and worried as if she'd lost her best friend. Unfortunately, she might have.

They drove back to her condo in silence, and he quickly searched the rooms to make sure Simpleton hadn't been there while they were gone. They'd picked up burgers on their way back, but Lenora rushed upstairs to shower first.

Seeing that house had really upset her. He certainly understood.

He glanced out the back window, watching the trees sway in the wind. He found a couple of bottles of beer in her refrigerator and carried them along with the food upstairs, then stepped through the hall door to the terrace.

The fresh air reminded him of his ranch. Maybe he'd suggest they go there tomorrow.

What would she think of his property? The house needed updating, but it was a big homey farmhouse with a wraparound porch that offered an expansive view of the ranch and creek. At night he enjoyed sitting outside, listening to the sounds of crickets chirping and the horses galloping in the pasture. Most folks hated the rain, but he loved the way it scented the air and turned everything a vivid green.

The shower water kicked off, and he imagined Lenora stepping from the shower, all naked and wet and . . . beautiful. He closed his eyes, willing his libido under control.

Ever since he'd met her, he'd admired her, felt compassion for her. But deep down his feelings ran deeper. She was the first woman he'd ever known who stirred a longing for more than a night in her bed.

The terrace door opened, and he glanced up to see Lenora standing in the middle of the French doors from her bedroom. Her damp hair hung in long wavy tendrils around her face; her skin glowed pink from the hot shower.

She wasn't dressed provocatively, just a pair of cotton paja-ma shorts and a T-shirt, but she looked so damn sexy that she took his breath away.

His sex hardened as desire heated his blood, the need to pull her in his arms strong, but he reached for his beer instead.

Anything to distract him from the ache in his body and the longing in his heart.

———

LENORA'S BODY TINGLED AT the way Micah looked at her. For a brief second, she thought she saw desire.

As if he wanted to kiss her.

Delicious sensations skittered through her at the thought.

How long had it been since she'd actually wanted to be with a man?

Since before the attack . . .

She'd wondered if she'd ever want a man again. If she'd ever be normal.

But Micah was different. He was strong and compassionate. A protector.

Her protector.

He'd stood beside her five years ago, and he was beside her now.

But when the case ended, he would leave . . .

If ever she wanted to have the chance to hold him, to be with him, it was now.

"I hope you don't mind, I found a couple of beers and brought them up."

"That sounds great." Lenora accepted the bottle, turned it up and took a sip. The cold liquid soothed her parched throat and helped her to relax.

He shifted and looked at the table where he'd set the burgers. "You hungry?"

She was, but she wanted him. Wanted to be in his arms. Wanted him to hold her.

Instead, she nodded, and they sat down and ate. She picked at her food, thoughts of Nan and the bones in the basement taunting her. What if those belonged to another woman? Maybe one of Simpleton's victims they didn't know about?

"Lenora," Micah said softly. "Put it out of your mind for a while."

"I'm trying," she said as she sipped her beer. "But it's difficult."

He laid his hand against her cheek. "I'm sorry."

"I'm just glad you're here," she said, her voice a little huskier than she'd intended.

His gaze met hers, heat flickering in the dark depths. "I wish I could do more. I want him out of your life for good so you can move on."

She wanted that, too. Maybe Micah could help her move on. Could help her forget . . .

Guilt clawed at her. How could she think such selfish thoughts when her friend's life was in danger? When she might be enduring some horrific torture at that very moment?

Micah recognized the guilt in Lenora's eyes. He hated the waiting and wished to hell he had another clue to chase down, but he didn't, dammit. Maybe tech would send that map of places to check as possible hideouts soon.

"Lenora?"

She tossed her trash into the trashcan by the door. Night had set in, the moon a distant sliver above the woods. If they weren't plagued by the shadow of death, it might be a romantic night.

"I'm so worried about Nan," she finally said. "What if we don't find her in time? Even if she survives, she's going to hate me."

Micah couldn't resist. The last thing Lenora needed to do was torture herself with self-recriminations. He pulled her toward him, his voice low, soothing.

"This is not your fault," he said. He'd told her that before, and he'd keep telling her until he convinced her.

"But—"

"No buts, Lenora. We'll find him." He stroked her arms with his hands, and she gazed into his eyes as if weighing his words and trying to believe him.

Then she parted her lips with a sultry sigh, and his body hardened. He wanted to kiss her.

"Micah, thank you for being so understanding. I know you're just doing your job—"

"You're more than a job to me," he said, his voice husky.

The moment he said the words, he knew they were true. But he shouldn't have said them.

The last thing Lenora needed was pressure.

"I am?"

The vulnerability in her voice tore at him. "Yes. I admire you ... I want to protect you." The spark of sexuality in her eyes nearly sent him over the edge.

"I want to hold you."

A soft smile lit her eyes, and she slid her arms beneath his and stepped closer to him. "I want that, too."

He inhaled her sweet scent as she laid her head against his chest. He wrapped his arms around her and cradled her to him, savoring the fact that she trusted him.

A second later, she raised one hand and pressed it against his cheek. Her eyes glittered with hunger, making his blood go hot, and he lowered his head and kissed her.

One taste and he wanted more.

Lenora captured his face closer, and he deepened the kiss, exploring her mouth with his tongue as she parted her lips for him. He trailed his hands down her back and drew her closer to him, his hands itching to strip her and feel her naked body next to his.

She must have read his mind because she trailed kisses down his neck and one by one pulled at the buttons of his shirt, her nails scraping his hot, bare skin.

"Lenora?" He paused, desperate for control. But the feel of her lips on his heated skin was so erotic it was hard to remember why he shouldn't rush to take her to bed.

"Don't you want me, Micah?"

His heart thumped offbeat, and he threaded his hand in her hair and tilted her head so she would look at him. "Of course, I do. But I don't want to pressure you—"

She touched his lips with one finger to silence him. "You aren't, Micah. I ..." She ran her hand down his chest. "I want this."

A smile curved his mouth. "Are you sure?" He kissed her forehead, then her eyelids. "Because if you want to stop at any point, all you have to do is say so."

Her hands stroked his chest, teasing, inviting more play. "I won't. I trust you."

Emotions he'd never expected to feel bombarded him. Lenora's trust in him was just as important as having her.

And dammit, he wanted her with every fiber of his being.

CHAPTER 11

Lenora's breath rasped out as Micah moved toward the door to the bedroom. "Out here," she whispered, a seed of panic sprouting at being closed inside.

A sexy smile lit his eyes. "Whatever you want, Lenora."

His heady tone turned her heart inside out. Heaven help her, but she could fall in love with this man.

His tenderness as he lowered his head and dropped kisses along her jaw and neck made her shiver.

He removed his gun and holster and placed it on the table.

"Are you cold?" he asked huskily.

"No," she whispered. "Just excited."

His eyes darkened with longing and raw hunger. "Me, too." He ran a finger along her cheek. "I've wanted you for a long time. But I don't want to do anything to hurt you. I would never hurt you."

"I know. " She lifted his hand and kissed his palm tenderly. "You won't hurt me, Micah. You make me feel more alive than I have in ages."

"You don't know what your trust means to me," he murmured.

Tears threatened, but she blinked them away. She'd cried enough for a lifetime. She wouldn't let tears ruin this moment.

He traced a finger down her spine, his other hand sliding from her neck to her chest, and she kissed him again, moaning when his fingers danced around to touch her breast. Her nipples instantly stiffened to peaks, achy and needy, and she clung to him, silently begging him for more.

He ran his hands down her hips, then gently carried her to the chaise. She shoved the blanket aside as he laid her down. His look was one of greed mixed with such hunger that she instantly pulled him on top of her.

"You are the sexiest man I've ever known," she whispered. "Kiss me, Micah. Touch me all over."

His hair brushed her cheek as he nuzzled her neck, then he slowly slid his hands to the bottom of her T-shirt and tugged it over her head. Cool night air slid over her, making her draw him close again.

But she remembered the nasty scar and froze.

He braced himself on his hands and looked down at her with questions in his eyes.

"The scar," she said. "It's so ugly."

"There is nothing ugly about you," he said hoarsely as he kissed the sensitive skin between her breasts. "You're the most beautiful, desirable woman I've ever met."

Emotions swelled inside her, and she inhaled his masculine scent. He was so tender and strong that all her reservations fled.

"You feel wonderful," she said softly.

He kissed her again and slowly stripped his shirt, the primal gleam in his eyes making her body tingle all over. His chest was broad, muscular, his stomach flat, dark hair dusting his torso.

She raked her hands over him, watching anxiously as he removed his jeans. His black boxers did nothing to hide the thick erection jutting out.

For a moment, she swallowed, bitter memories trying to destroy her pleasure.

"Lenora?" He folded her hand in his and kissed each finger. "Look at me. It's just the two of us here. Me. You. No one else."

She latched onto his words and the sensual promises in his tone. "No one else."

Her breasts were exposed, felt heavy, aching. She laid his hand over one of them and smiled as he dipped his head to tug one turgid nipple into his mouth. He suckled her until she cried out his name and pushed at his boxers.

A low, sexy chuckle rumbled from his chest, and he lifted himself enough to shuck his boxers. Then he slowly peeled her pajama bottoms down her legs. She kicked them off, frantic to have him closer. To fill her.

To finally give her the pleasure that only Micah could give her.

MICAH'S HEART WAS POUNDING. He'd never second-guessed himself in the lovemaking department, but he'd never actually cared about his lover in a serious way.

What if he did something wrong? What if he did hurt her?

But Lenora raked her hand down to cup his throbbing cock, and he moaned.

Not yet, he told himself. He had to pleasure her first. Erase all the violent memories.

They could do fast and furious the next time.

Next time? Was he thinking about having her again?

She squeezed his thick length, and he swallowed back a moan. Yes, he would have her again.

Shifting to control himself, he trailed kisses down her breasts again, circling each nipple with his tongue, then teasing her over and over until she lifted her hips in invitation.

His blood was so hot he thought he might explode, but he slid down her body, parted her legs and dipped his head to taste her. Lenora moaned, whispering his name, as he flicked his tongue out to tease her, and a sigh of pure erotic pleasure flowed from her lips.

She tasted like sweetness and honey, arousing his primal needs. He swirled his tongue around her feminine lips, then thrust it inside her.

She groaned again and clenched the chaise with her fingers as her body quivered with her release.

"Micah . . ."

His cock heavy with the need to be inside her, he slid up her body and teased her with the tip. "Lenora?"

"I want this, Micah," she whispered with the most heart-breakingly, beautiful smile he'd ever seen. "I want you inside me."

Her husky words almost sent him over the edge. But he wanted them to ride the waves of pleasure together

He'd also promised to protect her. Remembering a condom, he grabbed one from his jeans pocket and rolled it on.

Slowly he eased his length inside her.

She spread her legs wider, her body so tight that he withdrew, waiting to make sure she was ready. She quickly took his erection in her hand and guided him back to her.

He joined their bodies again, creating a sensual rhythm, rocking and thrusting until he filled her completely, and she cried out his name in another explosive orgasm.

Sensations flooded him, and he moaned and kissed her neck as he came inside her.

They lay together panting and sated, wrapped in each other's arms for several minutes. Finally, he rose, discarded the condom and lay back down beside her. When he pulled her in his arms, he kissed her again, his heart squeezing as she stroked his chest and sighed in contentment.

He'd never made love to any woman with such passion. With such emotion.

How in the hell was he going to walk away from her when the case was over?

⸻

LENORA HAD NEVER FELT so sated and peaceful in her life. Micah's sexy scent and touch twisted her heart into knots.

She was falling in love with him.

Fear of heartbreak hit her, but she tamped it down. She'd suffered the worst imaginable horrors during her abduction.

She would survive when Micah left.

After all, heartbreak couldn't kill her. Could it?

Micah's breathing turned slow and steady, and she realized he'd fallen asleep. She fell asleep, too, dreaming of Micah and being together forever.

But sometime later, the buzzing of a phone jerked her from her peace. She frowned and turned over, wondering if it was Micah's. But it was her phone vibrating from the table.

Slowly she extracted herself from Micah's arms, missing him already as she tiptoed over to retrieve it. Frowning when she saw *Unknown* on the screen, she punched connect.

The sound of a wheezed breath made her heart stop. "Lenora . . . stay away," her mother screamed. "Don't do what he says."

Icy fear paralyzed her. "Mother?"

"He's got me, but don't give in to him."

Her mother's scream followed . . .

"Mom?" Lenora choked on the word, her knees buckling.

Simpleton's monstrous voice replied, "If you want to see your mother and friend alive, come to me. And come alone."

Lenora bit back a sob and glanced at Micah who looked so sexy and heavenly naked on her chaise that she wanted to fall into his arms again. He would protect her, save her mother and Nan.

"If you bring that fucking cop, everyone dies," Simpleton growled. "Including your lover boy."

Lenora gasped and scanned the woods beyond the terrace. How could he possibly know she'd slept with Micah? Was he watching her?

She inhaled for courage. "Just tell me where to meet you."

"Go down the stairs and get in the car. I'll text you an address."

Lenora tiptoed to the French doors just as the phone went silent. Tears blurred her vision as she yanked a pair of jeans and a T-shirt from the closet and hurriedly dressed. Then she grabbed her gun from the drawer where she'd hidden it and jammed it in her purse.

She was reaching for her keys when suddenly she felt someone behind her.

"Where the hell do you think you're going?"

She winced, desperate to tell Micah. Desperate to save him.

She couldn't live with herself if he died because of her.

"I just needed some air, to think," she hedged.

"There's air on your terrace." Micah spun her around to face him. His eyes looked feral. "What's going on, Lenora?"

"I . . . it . . . was just too much," she said, lying. "I need to be alone for a while."

He stared at her for a minute, disappointment in his expression. "Then I'll go downstairs."

"Just leave, go home," she cried. "I don't want you here anymore."

"You may regret making love to me, but I'm not leaving you alone, not while that maniac is out there."

Lenora trembled. "Please, Micah, just go . . ."

"No." He glanced down and saw the phone in her hands. A muscle ticked in his jaw as reality dawned, and he jerked it from her. "He called you, didn't he?"

She bit her tongue as Micah checked the caller ID log. He flipped it around to confront her. "There it is, an *Unknown*."

"Micah, please let me handle this."

"What did he say, Lenora?"

Anger shot through her. "He has my mother." Her voice cracked. "For God's sake, Micah, I have to go and I have to do it alone or he'll kill her."

He would probably kill her anyway. Kill them all. But she had to try to save them.

"Where did he tell you to come?"

"He's going to text the address to me." She jerked the phone from his hand, jammed it in her pocket and reached for her keys. "Now, let me go."

He pulled her back into his arms. Terrified for Nan and her mother, she pushed at his chest, but he wrapped his arms so tightly around her that she couldn't move.

"You are not going alone, Lenora. He'll kill all of you. I can't let that happen."

"Please, Micah," she whispered. "My mother . . ."

"I know, baby, I know." He pressed a kiss in her hair and she fell apart. For a full minute, she allowed herself to cry. He rocked her in his arms, soothing her. When she finally took a breath, he framed her face with his hands.

"Listen to me. I'll hide in the back. He won't know I'm even there until I jump out and surprise him."

"He knows about you, us. What if something goes wrong?"

"I'll text my partner and tell him to keep a trace on my phone. He'll know where we are and have back-up waiting."

A war raged in her mind, but she finally agreed. She didn't want Micah to get killed, but she was terrified for her mother and friend.

He threw on his clothes, holstered his weapon, and they hurried downstairs together. He called his partner as she reached for the door. As soon as he set up the trace, he nodded for her to go outside.

She stepped on the front stoop and headed toward her car. Micah followed her, but a shot rang out behind her.

She screamed and spun around just as Micah hit the ground. A second later, Simpleton grabbed her and shoved a gun to her back.

"Get in and drive, Lenora. It's time we got the party started. Sorry to say but lover boy won't be joining us."

CHAPTER 12

MICAH ROUSED FROM UNCONSCIOUSNESS, dragged himself up from the ground, and pressed a hand to his shoulder where the bastard had shot him. Blood oozed from the wound, but he didn't have time to deal with it.

Simpleton was getting away with Lenora.

He pulled a handkerchief from his pocket, tucked it inside his shirt to absorb the blood, then called his buddy, Mitchell.

"He has Lenora, Mitch. I need your help."

"What can I do?"

"Get an APB out on Lenora's car." He gave him the make and license plate. "I'm phoning the tech team now for those locations to check out."

"I'll get on the APB and pick you up at the ranch with the chopper."

Micah ended the call, then phoned tech.

The analyst cleared his throat. "I was just about to email you the map and coordinates of the areas we narrowed down."

"Send it now. Simpleton has Lenora. I have to hurry."

He hung up, rushed inside the condo, hurried into the bathroom, dug under Lenora's sink and found gauze and tape. Pain shot through his shoulder as he stripped his shirt and examined the wound. Dammit, the bullet had lodged inside.

Too deep for him to remove himself. Besides, he didn't have time.

He poured antiseptic on the wound, gritting his teeth as he cleaned it. Blood still oozed from the bullet hole, but he applied pressure with some gauze, tossed the bloody gauze away, then packed it with more gauze. Using his teeth, he ripped off tape and wrapped it around the gauze and his shoulder, securing it tightly to keep the pressure on his injury.

His phone dinged that the email was coming through from the tech. Three different areas, all near small private airfields.

From the topography maps and photographs, there were two different Victorian houses that had been abandoned in isolated areas near airfields.

Was Simpleton taking Lenora to one of them?

It was a long shot, but the only lead he had.

Pulse hammering, he jogged outside to his SUV, jumped in and drove to his ranch.

The few minutes it took him to get there felt like an eternity. Every second he imagined Simpleton with his hands on Lenora.

He was going to kill the creep.

He barreled up the drive, the sight of his ranch house usually a welcome reprieve from the ugliness of his job. Yet tonight, he couldn't enjoy it.

He threw the SUV into park, relieved to see Mitch waiting by the chopper, and hit the ground running.

"The APB's been issued," Mitch said. "Do you have a place to start?"

"A couple, yeah. Let's go."

He jumped in the chopper and Mitch fired it up. A second later, they were flying across the treetops. He watched the horses running in the pasture freely and vowed Lenora would see this place soon.

She had to.

He couldn't bear it if he lost her.

Lenora clenched the steering wheel in a white-knuckled grip. "Did you hurt my mother?"

Simpleton waved the gun at her. He'd already confiscated hers, dammit.

"I'll let Mommy tell you what we did together," he said in a singsong voice.

Revulsion seized Lenora. She wanted to kill this man more than she'd ever imagined possible. The thought of his hands on her mother, on Nan . . .

She blinked to make the images disappear. She had to focus. Figure out a way to save the three of them.

And Micah . . . God, what if he was dead? She'd heard that gunshot. He'd gone down. And she'd seen blood pooling on the ground.

What if he didn't make it?

For now, she was on her own. There was no one to save Nan and her mother but her.

Simpleton had taken everything from her once.

Not this time.

"Turn there," he growled.

She swerved onto a side road that looked as if it led to nowhere. Darkness shrouded the woods and land, the sounds of silence along the deserted road eerie and unnerving.

"Is Nan still alive?"

He rubbed a hand over his head. He looked so different from when she'd last seen him that she barely recognized him. He was leaner, more muscled up. He'd had scraggly hair and a beard when he was arrested. The mustache and fake sideburns made his face appear longer. But his eyes still glittered with the same evil that had dominated his expression when he'd held her captive. And the skull and snake tattoos on his head and face made him look even more menacing.

She shivered. No matter what abuse he'd suffered as a child, he was evil. Pure evil.

"Alive and waiting on you."

Lenora considered ramming the car into a tree to shut him up. Maybe the impact would kill him. It might kill her, too, but it would be worth it to stop him from hurting anyone else.

But if she did, she might never find Nan and her mother.

She slanted him a hate-filled look. "What did you do to her?"

He traced a finger along her cheek. "Tsk, tsk, tsk, my sweet Lenora. We'll all be together soon enough."

She swallowed in disgust but didn't comment. Instead, she took the turn to the left that he pointed out, driving them deeper and deeper into the bowels of the woods and the horrors that waited for her.

"THERE." MICAH POINTED TO a section of land by the river. "There's supposedly an old house that matches the description near that ravine.

Mitch scanned the area, searching for a place to land the chopper. "There are too many damn trees."

"How about to the right?" Micah suggested. "If you can't set it down, you can drop me and I'll hike in on foot."

"Let me try it first." Mitch expertly guided the helicopter over a dense patch of woods, then lowered it onto the ground. As soon as he cut the engine, Micah jumped out. His shoulder throbbed like the devil, but at least the bleeding had slowed.

Micah checked the map and led the way along the river using his flashlight and compass to guide them. They hiked through patches of briars and over tree stumps, the scent of wet earth and moss mingling with the stench of a dead animal.

Praying this was the spot, Micah jogged along the creek until he spotted the old house in the distance. He sped up, drawing his gun and searching the area for signs indicating Simpleton had been near the house.

When he reached a clearing in front of the place, he hesitated, using his binoculars to get a better view.

"See anything?" Mitch asked in a low voice.

"Not yet." Micah spanned the front of the house, then the sides but didn't find a car or any sign of life. "Simpleton may not have gotten back with Lenora yet."

Or they could be at the wrong place, wasting precious time . . .

They wove through the trees, inching up to the front door. Micah checked the windows, but they were either locked or painted shut. The house was rotting, paint peeling off, revealing evidence of raccoons nesting and trashing the place.

Mitch gestured that he'd look around back, and Micah jiggled the front door. It stuck, but he managed to pry it open. The inside was dark, cold, and smelled like rotten food and mold.

He shined his flashlight inside, boards screeching beneath his boots as he entered. Unlike Simpleton's childhood home, this one was deserted, had no furniture. He made his way to the kitchen and saw no evidence anyone had been there.

Mitch crept inside, his gun at the ready.

"Nothing in here. You search the upstairs, I'll look for a basement," Micah said.

Micah slipped into the hallway while Mitch headed up the back staircase. He aimed the flashlight into the hall and found a door leading to the downstairs. Once again, Micah was pitched into darkness, but he used his flashlight to illuminate his way. Midway, he paused and waved the light across the dark cement room. In one corner, he noticed shelves filled with dented canned goods and canning jars. A rusted lawn mower and gardening tools that hadn't been used in ages filled another corner.

Simpleton wasn't here.

"Nan? Mrs. Lockhart?" His voice echoed in the emptiness. But he crept down the rest of the steps then searched the basement for a hidden door or room.

Nothing.

Disappointment ballooned in his chest, and he quickly raced back up to the main floor. Mitch met him in the foyer.

"Nothing up there."

"Nothing in the basement either." They needed to check the other site.

His phone buzzed, and he snatched it up. "Hardin."

Lt. Roper's voice. "Micah, we got a call. Simpleton ditched the truck he was driving. We caught him on tape stealing a black Honda from the parking lot of a convenience store near Dry Creek Run."

Micah glanced at the map on his phone. One of the houses on his list was off that road. "Thanks. I'm on my way."

"What?" Mitch asked.

"Let's go. Simpleton was spotted near Dry Creek Run Road."

They jogged toward the chopper and lifted off again. Mitch hit the air at full speed, soaring over treetops, then the main highway until they veered onto a dirt road.

Tension knotted Mitch's shoulders as he looked through his night binoculars in search of Simpleton's vehicle and the house. An eternity later, he spotted the Victorian place nestled in the woods.

The Honda was parked at an odd angle in the yard, the door left ajar.

"There it is," he said, adrenaline kicking in.

"I'll have to look for a spot to land."

"Drop me, then you can find a landing spot and meet me there. We can't waste any time. Simpleton could be torturing Lenora right now."

"I HAVE TO SEE my mother," Lenora said as Simpleton pushed her down the stairs. Just like before, the basement was dark. Dank, musky odors assaulted her, her breath shaky in the silence.

"Mom? Nan?"

"Lenora, run!" her mother shouted.

"Help!" Nan yelled.

Simpleton's laughter boomed around her. Then he shoved her toward a white porcelain tub that gleamed below a low hanging light. Ice cubes floated in the water, waiting for her.

The memory of his torture taunted her. She would not go down without a fight this time.

He poked the gun in her back, and she pivoted toward him. "Let them go, and I'll do anything you want."

"You're going to do that anyway."

She softened her voice. "I'll go away with you. Just the two of us. Then you can have me all the time." She forced herself to run her finger along his cheek. "Don't you want that, Robert?" His first name tasted like acid on her tongue.

His eyes glittered with evil as he studied her. Then he jerked her hand away and dragged her toward the tub. "Nice try, but you have to be punished. I can still smell that bastard's sex on you."

Lenora gritted her teeth. At least if she died, she had the memory of Micah's tender lovemaking to hold onto.

Simpleton aimed the gun at her chest. "Take off your clothes."

Lenora quickly scanned the room for a weapon, anything to use to fight him. But the room held nothing useful. She only saw the two rooms holding his hostages.

Her belt.

She slowly unbuckled the belt and eased it through the belt loops. She had one chance, and she had to take it. She gripped it in her hand, swung it up and hit him in the face.

He yelped in pain as the buckle hit his cheekbone. She took advantage of his shock to knock the gun from his hand.

He bellowed in anger, grabbed her arm then slung her toward the floor. She grunted, but recovered and stabbed his eyes with her fingers. When he staggered backward, she darted toward the gun.

But he caught her around the neck with his hands, then dragged her toward the tub.

She screamed, biting at his arms and kicking with all her might.

But he was stronger, clenched her around the waist and pushed her over the side of the tub, then shoved her head down into the icy water.

CHAPTER 13

THE SOUND OF LENORA'S scream made Micah's blood run cold. He tiptoed toward the basement stairs, his pulse drumming like a jackhammer.

He had to save Lenora.

Holding his breath, he eased open the door, then crept down the dark stairs. The sound of shuffling, then another scream rent the air, and he braced his gun, slowly inching his way down each step until he spotted Simpleton shoving Lenora's head into a tub of water.

Sick fucker.

"Let her go," he growled as his boots hit the bottom step.

Simpleton jerked his head up, his smile gleaming in the semidarkness. "Come any closer and she's dead."

Lenora kicked and tried to pry the bastard's hands off her neck as she flailed, head immersed in the ice bath. Screams and pounding echoed from two rooms behind them. The rooms where he'd obviously locked Nan and Lenora's mother.

"Let her go or I'll drop you like a rock," Micah said.

He spotted Simpleton's gun on the chair near the tub. He had to release one hand from Lenora's neck to retrieve it. "You won't take me in alive," Simpleton said.

Micah grinned although he was counting the seconds Lenora had been under water. "Dead's fine with me."

Simpleton shoved her deeper with one hand and stretched to grab his gun.

Micah didn't hesitate. He fired a round into the man's chest. Simpleton grunted and staggered back. Micah strode across the room and fired, again and again, filling the man's chest with bullets.

Simpleton collapsed backward, blood spurting as he gurgled for air. Lenora jerked her head up, gasping for a breath.

He raced to her and dragged her in his arms. She clutched his shoulders, her body trembling. Her cheeks were chilled and red, her hair damp. He stroked her back to warm her, giving her time to shed her emotions.

Simpleton tried to rally, his hands clawing for help to get up, but Micah pointed the gun at him again. The man's eyes bulged, and blood dripped from his mouth, then his body convulsed and went limp.

"He's dead, Lenora," he murmured.

She exhaled shakily, then looked up at him. Her eyes were slightly glazed, but as she refocused, fear flared in her eyes. "My mother! Nan!"

He gently released her, and she raced to the first room while he rushed to the second. "We need a key for the padlocks," she cried.

Micah scanned the room, then spotted a set of keys on the floor beside Simpleton. He grabbed them, tried one, then the other until he unlocked the first room.

"Mom!" Lenora cried.

Lenora rushed inside and helped her mother out while he rescued Nan. Both women looked terrified and were sobbing, their hands bound. Micah quickly used his knife to free them.

Lenora's mother fell into Lenora's arms, and Nan joined them just as Mitch raced down the stairs. "We need an ambulance," Micah said, noting the bruises on Nan's arms and legs.

"I'll phone it in." Mitch made the call while Micah strode to Simpleton to make sure he was dead and would never be coming back.

LENORA COULDN'T STOP SHIVERING. The icy water must have frozen her from the inside out. She wrapped the blanket tighter around her shoulders though and went to the doctor to ask about her mother.

The ambulance ride had been trying. Tense. Alternately quiet and filled with sobs as Nan and her mother poured out their rage and terror. Apparently, Nan had suffered the most. The icy dunks in the bath, a beating, and a near rape. For some reason, Simpleton had stopped just before penetration, saying he wanted to let Lenora watch the fun.

Her mother had been emotionally terrorized, but he hadn't touched her. Again, he wanted Lenora to watch.

Thankfully, Micah had arrived in time.

How, she had no idea. The man had been shot, but he'd ignored his own injuries to save her and the people she loved.

The doctor approached her about Nan. "She's physically going to be okay. She'll need counseling and time, but she should recover fully."

Lenora thanked him then slipped into Nan's room. She'd been treated for minor abrasions and lay propped on a bed of pillows. When she saw Lenora, sorrow filled her face. "Lenora."

"I'm here," she said, quickly rushing to her friend's side. But she hesitated before touching her. "I'm so sorry, Nan. So sorry. This is my fault."

Nan shook her head. "No, I . . . shouldn't have turned away from you. It was . . . he was . . . horrible."

"I know." Lenora wiped a tear away. "I didn't think he'd come after you."

Nan stiffened her spine. "I'll be all right."

"But—"

"I know I'll need help to get over it," she said, her voice cracking, "but I won't let that sick creep destroy me. You survived much worse."

But had she? She still slept on the terrace because of the nightmares. Had she really moved on?

"Can you ever forgive me, Lenora?"

Lenora held out her arms, and the two of them hugged. Nan burst into tears, and Lenora soothed her friend as Micah had her, knowing more than anything that Nan needed loving support, not judgment or demands.

"Take all the time you need to recover," Lenora whispered. "I'm still working on that myself."

Nan nodded against her, and they stayed in each other's arms for a long time. Finally, the nurse stepped in to give Nan a sedative to help her sleep.

"I'll be back," Lenora said. "I'm here for you, Nan. Whatever you need. All you have to do is call."

"I know, thanks." Nan hugged the covers to her and gave her a small smile of courage as Lenora left the room.

Lenora walked across the hall and peeked in on her mother. "Are you all right, Mom?"

"I will be," her mother said with a tilt to her chin. "I . . . I'm so sorry, honey."

"Sorry for what?" Lenora said softly.

"For not understanding before."

Tears pricked at Lenora's eyes as she rushed to her mother and cradled her hands in hers. "Mom, you were there for me. I know that, but it was just difficult for me to talk about what happened. I was ashamed. I felt like I'd done something to deserve what happened."

"Oh, no, sweetheart, never think that." A tear trickled down her mother's cheek. "I should have encouraged you to talk, but it hurt so badly to know what he did to you. I felt . . . helpless. I'm your mother. Mothers are supposed to protect their children." Sorrow laced her shaky voice. "I wanted to take away your pain, and I couldn't."

Lenora sniffled and leaned over to hug her mother. "We both did the best we could." She choked back a sob, then stroked her mother's hair from her cheek. "I just want you to be okay."

"I will be," her mother said. "Now that horrid man is dead."

Lenora squeezed her mother's hand. "I have to admit I'm glad he is."

They hugged again, then Lenora sat by her mother's bed until she fell asleep.

When she walked out of the room, Micah was waiting, his expression concerned. "Are you all right?"

"I should ask you that. You were shot."

He shrugged, indicating his sling. "Doc removed the bullet, gave me some pain meds. I'm good. Oh, by the way, forensics identified the body in Simpleton's old house. It was his father. Theory is that the mother killed him."

He winced, and Lenora's nerves fluttered.

She wanted to hug him, to hold him, to beg him to come home with her. But he'd almost died because of her just as Nan and her mother had.

How could any of them ever forgive her?

MICAH SAW THE WHEELS turning in Lenora's pretty head. Guilt. Regret. Concern about everyone but herself.

So like Lenora.

"Come on. I'll take you home."

Lenora arched a brow. "I thought you were on pain meds."

A smile tugged at his lips. "I said the doc gave them to me. Didn't say I took any of them."

Lenora smiled. "Then let's go so you can get some rest."

He placed his hand at her back, and they walked outside together.

"How's Nan and your mother?" he asked as he pulled away from the hospital.

"They're going to be okay, I think."

Micah's fingers tightened around the steering wheel. "You know right now they're high on adrenaline, relieved we found them. But they'll have moments."

"I know," Lenora said softly. "There will be bad days. Nights. Nightmares. It will be a process. But I'll be there for them."

"You are amazing," he said.

"I . . . I'm just grateful that you saved us."

She shivered again, and he ached to pull her up against him, but she leaned against the door, hugging the blanket they'd given her at the hospital around her and closed her eyes.

Twenty minutes later, they arrived at her condo, and he walked her to the door.

Lenora turned to him, her eyes glittering with emotions. "Thank you for everything, Micah."

He swallowed, tempted to say he'd only been doing his job. But that was a lie. It had been personal with Lenora ever since the start.

He tucked a strand of her damp hair behind her ear, the memory of seeing Simpleton shoving her head under water reminding him of the terror he'd felt at the thought of losing her.

"I'm just sorry that—"

"No regrets." She stroked his cheek with her fingers. "You kept your promise, Micah. I'll never forget that."

It sounded as if she was saying goodbye. He knew she'd been through hell tonight. He should leave her and let her rest.

"Will you be all right tonight?" he asked softly.

She offered him a brave smile. "He's dead. You killed him. I should be."

Their gazes locked for a moment, and his hands itched to pull her up against him and kiss her. But she'd been mauled by another man tonight.

He couldn't pressure her.

"Lock the door and call me if you need me."

She gave a small nod, her eyes flickering with emotions he couldn't quite define. Deciding she needed time, he turned and walked to his SUV.

But just as he reached for the door, his cell phone rang. Figuring it was the lieutenant tying up the case, he hit connect.

"Sgt. Hardin."

Lenora's soft voice echoed over the line, "I need you."

Perspiration exploded on his brow as he glanced back at the doorway. Lenora stood in the threshold holding the phone, looking vulnerable and scared and so damn beautiful that his knees felt weak.

Desire and hunger shot through him as he slowly walked up to her. "Lenora?"

"I don't want to be alone tonight."

His voice turned husky with relief and passion. "Me, neither."

"I know you're injured."

His mouth twitched. He didn't give a damn about his stitches. "I can still hold you."

She gave him a sultry smile and held out her hand, and he followed her inside.

He paused at her bedroom, one hand on her cheek. "Are you sure, Lenora?"She nodded. "I'm sure I want you."

His breath caught in his throat. "What if I said I love you?"

She licked her lips, and to his delight, pulled him toward her. "Then I'd say I love you back."

He reached down to lift her in his arms but winced when his stitches pulled. She laughed and tugged his hand, and they hurried into the bedroom together.

EPILOGUE

Six months later

LENORA FLUFFED HER VEIL as she examined her reflection in the mirror. She'd been planning weddings and happily-ever-afters for others for years, never expecting to find her own.

But now she had, she couldn't wait to say her vows to Micah.

Her mother poked her head into the extra bedroom where she was getting ready. Micah had brought her to the ranch for a few days after Simpleton's death, and she'd fallen in love with the land.

She and Jenny had planned the wedding on the front lawn at sunset. White draped chairs and tables were set up facing a gazebo situated on the small hill that overlooked the creek.

"You look beautiful, honey." Her mother fastened a silver locket around her neck. "Here is your something borrowed."

Lenora fingered the heart with appreciation. The necklace had been passed down through several generations. "Thank you, Mom. I'm glad you're here."

"And I'm happy you found such a wonderful man."

Lenora blinked back emotions. She refused to cry today. She and her mother and Nan had already shed way too many tears. Both of them had agreed to counseling and were healing. Nan admitted she still had nightmares, but they were happening less frequently. Ironically, the ordeal had brought the two of them closer again.

Jenny and Nan slipped into the room, both looking gorgeous in the classic black dresses they'd chosen as bridesmaids.

"It's time," Nan squealed.

Jenny squeezed her hand. "Everything looks perfect. Including you."

Lenora hugged them both.

"The music's beginning." Her mother clapped her hands. "Let's go, girls."

Jenny opened the door and ushered Nan and Lenora's mother outside to be seated. Lenora followed, her bridal gown swishing as she made her way to the French doors overlooking the lawn.

Jenny's fiancé Troy played the guitar, strumming softly as the bridesmaids walked through the center aisle between the rows of chairs lined up for the guests.

The bridal march began, and she spotted Micah, dressed in a long western duster and black Stetson, waiting for her in front of the gazebo.

He looked so sexy and handsome that her heart nearly burst with joy.

As she walked down the aisle toward him, images of their future together flashed in her mind, making her heart pound with anticipation. When she reached him, she handed Jenny her bouquet of roses and took Micah's hand.

The Reverend, an older man she'd met through her job, had taken a special interest in her mother at the rehearsal. Maybe her mother would have a second chance at love now.

He greeted everyone and read a Bible verse, but she and Micah had chosen to write their own vows.

Micah began. "Lenora, I thought by working in law enforcement that I had to be alone. But you taught me that love means more than a job. That my job means nothing without you. I am so blessed to have you as my bride."

Lenora stared into his eyes, touched by his heartfelt words. "Micah, I once lived in a world of darkness. But the day you took my hand and walked me back into the light, I fell in love with you. I loved you then, I love you now, I'll love you forever."

They exchanged rings, and the reverend pronounced them husband and wife.

The ceremony was short and sweet, but Lenora knew in her heart that their marriage and their love would last a lifetime.

MICAH HAD NEVER EXPECTED to find a soul mate, but he'd found one in Lenora. He couldn't help but blush as he shook hands with his fellow rangers and watched the crowd disperse.

As much as he'd enjoyed the party and dancing with his bride, he was ready to be alone with his new wife.

And he still had a surprise for her.

She'd loved his ranch immediately and hadn't cared that it was rundown. But before he moved her here, he'd wanted to make some changes.

Lenora waved goodbye to her friends and mother, then sashayed over to him. "Hey, husband."

"Wife," he said with a grin. "I say we take this champagne inside."

She glanced at the fading sun on the horizon. "But I hate to leave this view."

"You won't miss it." He swung her up in his arms, grabbed the champagne and two flutes for her to hold then carried her inside to the master suite.

He'd insisted she redecorate the kitchen, but he'd kept her from the master suite to give him time to renovate it.

When he opened the door with his foot, she gasped. "Micah . . . it's beautiful."

He grinned. He'd knocked out the back wall and extended the room, added skylights, and French doors to offer a view of the sky and the sweeping land. The colors of the sunset shimmered on the horizon.

"You did this for me?" she whispered, awe in her voice.

"I know you don't like closed in spaces." He nuzzled her neck. "I wanted you to have your terrace and sunset here at our home."

"Thank you, Micah." Lenora clasped his face between her hands. "I love you. I always will."

"And I love you. You've given me everything I ever wanted."

She smiled and kissed him, and he laid her on the king sized sleigh bed he'd bought for them to share.

Smiling seductively, he stripped her wedding gown and his clothes, and they made love all night with the stars twinkling through the skylights and the moon glowing bright just as their love would glow the rest of their lives.

OTHER BOOKS

THE MANHUNT SERIES
Safe by His Side (Book 2)
Safe with Him (Book 3)

THE KEEPERS SERIES
Pretty Little Killers (Book 1)
Good Little Girls (Book 2)
Little White Lies (Prequel to Dead Little Darlings)
Dead Little Darlings (Book 3)

THE GRAVEYARD FALLS SERIES
All the Beautiful Brides (Book 1)
All the Pretty Faces (Book 2)
All the Dead Girls (Book 3)

THE SLAUGHTER CREEK SERIES
Before She Dies (Prequel)
Dying to Tell (Book 1)
Her Dying Breath (Book 2)
Worth Dying For (Book 3)
Dying for Love (Book 4)

THE DEMONBORN SERIES
Heartless (Book 1)
Mindless (Book 2)
Soulless (Book 3)

RITA'S LIGHTER SIDE
Marry Me, Maddie
Sleepless in Savannah
Love Me, Lucy
Husband Hunting 101
Here Comes the Bride
There Goes the Groom
Single and Searching
Under the Covers

ABOUT THE AUTHOR

USA Today AND AWARD-WINNING author Rita Herron fell in love with books at the ripe age of eight when she read her first Trixie Belden mystery. But she didn't think real people grew up to be writers, so she became a teacher instead. Now she writes so she doesn't have to get a real job!

With over ninety books to her credit, she's penned romantic suspense, romantic comedy, and YA stories, but she especially loves writing dark romantic suspense tales set in southern small towns.

For more on Rita and her titles, visit her at www.ritaherron.com. You can also follow her on Facebook and Twitter @ ritaherron.